# HER BILLIONAIRE
## COWBOY'S
### *Triplets*

# HER BILLIONAIRE COWBOY'S *Triplets*

## GALLOWAY SONS FARM
## CHRISTMAS IN FAIR CREEK, BOOK 2

# CATHY SHOUSE

*Her Billionaire Cowboy's Triplets*
Cathy Shouse

Interior design and formatting by
E.M.
TIPPETTS
BOOK DESIGNS

www.emtippettsbookdesigns.com

# Chapter 1

Kristin Barclay opened the heavy glass hospital door and entered next to the huge Christmas tree inside the lobby, wishing she were someplace else. Anywhere at all.

At least today's visit partly involved good news. She pulled her phone from her purse and made a call.

Mandi Bush picked up her phone. "Are you here?" Her voice was enthusiastic, even though they had only been acquaintances in a support group long ago and hadn't been in touch for years.

Kristin attempted to match the new mother's mood. "Yep. I just stepped inside. Should be in the maternity ward in a couple of minutes." She disconnected.

She turned off the main hallway and entered a private corridor which led into a viewing area where newborns were lined up in bassinets. Wrapped in red blankets made to look like Christmas stockings, wearing bright-green knitted caps, each baby had a card with their name on it nearby.

Mandi came in by the bassinets, grinning from ear to ear, and picked up baby Brent. She gestured for Kristin to meet her at the little side door.

Kristin plastered a smile on her face as she went to meet them, determined not to dwell on how many new babies she'd visited. One day, this might be her. Just maybe.

Mandi stepped into the small room, holding baby Brent.

Kristin studied the darling face and bright eyes. "He's perfect." He really was a pretty baby. "After all your years of infertility treatments, I'm so happy for you and Herb."

The first-time mom beamed and shifted her little bundle to her shoulder. "I saw the sign you're speaking at the infertility support group here. Thanks for answering a text from an old friend and stopping by. How are you and Craig doing?"

"Has it been that long since you guys moved away?" Kristin sighed. "Our infertility treatments were unsuccessful. We ended up getting divorced, and Craig passed away three years ago."

Mandi patted Brent's back. "I had no idea. I'm so sorry."

"Thanks. You know, God has a plan though. It's the strangest timing that you would get back in touch. Craig and I had three leftover embryos from our last IVF treatment I kept frozen in storage. I'm thirty-three, not getting any younger, and my doctor transferred them into my uterus last week." She'd made the decision to go through with a frozen embryo transplant after praying long and hard about it.

Mandi's eyes opened wide. "Good for you!" She shifted Brent to her other shoulder. "This little angel is from a frozen embryo transfer."

"Really? My chances of success aren't good, but when they wanted me to give mine away, donate them to science, or…. I knew I had to give them a chance. It felt like saving my family. Listen, I need to go and clear my head for this presentation." She turned toward the exit.

"And I better rest. Thanks for stopping by. I'll be praying for you. Remember, all babies are miracles."

Kristin waved before she went through the door and blew a kiss to mom and son. Once in the main corridor, she checked the wall clock. She was early, must have been anxious about seeing Mandi again and giving her talk to the support group.

She turned down the next hallway, and the strong scent of coffee wafted over as a customer exited a coffee shop door. She squeezed in through the half-open door, sending up a prayer of thanks. Relaxing for a few minutes was just what she needed.

This little break was a taste of what the Miracle Mommies House she was starting would offer. Women undergoing infertility treatments were going to be able to enjoy a little TLC, like mini retreats. They could join online or in person and reduce their stress levels, which played a role in some couples' failure to conceive.

Smelling the coffee was the closest she was going to get to it, unfortunately. "I'll have a hot chocolate with marshmallow and whipped cream," she told the barista. The doctor had said to be careful about everything until they knew the results of the procedure.

"Name?"

"Sam." Shortening her middle name for them spared her from having her first name misspelled, one of her pet peeves.

She paid and took a seat. Though Kristin was single, she'd continued attending infertility groups, to heal her pain and to support others.

A dark-haired man in a denim shirt and wearing a cowboy hat sat partly in shadow at a little corner table. Definitely not the type she usually spotted at the clinic. But cowboys were all over Fair Creek. This one had to be the best-looking one she'd seen.

Too bad she wasn't in the market.

He held a camera and radiated charisma as he gazed intently around the room, not seeming to miss a detail. Kristin tried to appear casual as she straightened up in her seat, just as his perusal landed on her. A smile crossed his face, and his white teeth with a slight gap in front managed to make him more attractive somehow. She smiled back, something she never did with random strangers.

The barista called, "Sam." When she sneaked another peek, the cowboy was leaning more into the light as he held the camera up to that handsome face and aimed at a set of drawings on the wall. He adjusted the lens with precise movements of his long, lean fingers.

*Snap out of it, Kristin.* She needed to get her drink.

Pushing herself up from the chair, she didn't feel quite right. When she sort of popped out of it, a light-headedness came over her. The sensation would pass. She sometimes got dizzy if she didn't eat right. She rested her hand on an arm of the chair to steady herself as tiny bright spots darted into her vision. Blinking her eyes slowly for a couple of seconds, only a few sparks of lightness behind her eyes remained so she proceeded toward the counter.

Partway there, she swayed on her feet. A strong arm slipped around her waist.

"Oh, I'm fine." *Fine as I'll ever be, anyway.*

"You're not usually fine?"

*Yikes.* Had she really said those words out loud? Better prove herself capable. She grabbed her drink so firmly that some sloshed out. An exact match of the other arm reached out, scooped up her drink for her, and started guiding her toward the back wall.

Sparks gone, she looked up. Up close, he took gorgeous to a new level—or three. She had been convinced she was beyond caring about appearance. But his thick, near-black hair, neat except for a stray thatch over one eyebrow, proved her wrong. Her mouth went dry.

Should have thrown on her new shirt this morning.

Where had that come from?

A glance at his maple-brown eyes was the best test of whether her vision had truly cleared. A flutter in her tummy confirmed her interest.

What was that?

She was pretty sure a woman with implanted embryos from her late ex-husband had no business developing a crush. Better embrace her recovery and leave the area. Now.

# Chapter 2

"I've got you." Leo Galloway kept a steadying grip on the blond's elbow in the hospital coffee shop to be sure she was really all right.

"I can take care of myself." But she stayed near enough for him to catch her if she did a repeat performance.

He'd left his iced coffee on the table with his camera while he went back to get a sweetener when she started to go down. Fortunately, his reflexes were good. Hard to say if she would've ended up on the floor.

She hadn't welcomed his help. It was okay by him if she liked doing things on her own. He admired her spunk. Carla, his ex, had been more than willing to lean on him—too willing—to have him save her. Not that breaking a nail while at a business conference or the smoothie store being closed when she drove up should rate as a crisis. But she'd taught him an independent woman would be a good thing in his book.

This woman's head came just above his shoulder, and he was six foot three. Wisps of her mid-length honey hair had briefly brushed his shirt. She had a sweet, melodious voice. He let go of her elbow but couldn't abandon her entirely, for some reason he couldn't explain. Her smile lit everything in the room except her eyes.

They reached his table, and he pulled out her chair, then sat opposite her. "You gave me a scare."

"All fine now."

"You're pale."

"I'm a rabid sunscreen user." She gave a grin, but it came off a little weak. "My friends used to tease me mercilessly after I'd given up on tanning, called me Casper. You know, the friendly ghost?"

"Some friends."

Her lips turned up, which made him feel better. "They meant it affectionately. I'm sorry for your trouble. I might have missed lunch…not sure about breakfast, either. Guess I fell off the bandwagon with my self-care routine."

He chuckled, stirred the sugar into his drink, and took a sip. "I'll get you one of those wraps?"

Her hand, delicate without seeming fragile, encircled her drink cup. "This'll do."

Something smelled extra sweet. "Is that hot chocolate? Don't you want me to get you something with a kick of caffeine at least?"

She dropped her chin and looked around as if to verify no one could eavesdrop on their conversation. According to the barista calling out her name, if Sam had something to hide, so did he. He'd come back to Fair Creek to his roots, to Galloway Sons Farm to comply with Dad's will. But he needed to get away from Boston for his own, medically advised reasons.

"My doctor doesn't want me to have coffee."

"Now that should be a criminal offense."

She just looked at him with those gorgeous blue eyes.

Why would she be off caffeine? One thing he and his ex-girlfriend had agreed on was not having kids. When she skipped her coffee and other weird things, turned out she was involved with someone else and wanted a family.

He swigged a gulp of his coffee. Since Carla, he hadn't had any interest in women.

The woman's gaze flicked to her phone. "I better get going." She stood up with ease, nice and steady. "You really know how to sweep a girl back onto her feet, you know that?"

"Well, you're not making my work easy. It's downright hard to help when you're bouncing back so quickly." He stood up slightly, as a farewell and to stop himself from doing something stupid he would regret. What had the barista called her? Oh, right. "See you around, Sam."

An unreadable expression came into her eyes and she sauntered off, leaving him smiling to himself. He had no doubt there was more to her than met the eye, which had been pleasing on its own.

His cup was empty, although he didn't remember drinking much during their conversation. Go figure. He gathered himself up, strung the camera strap around his neck, and walked away, tossing the cup into the nearest trash receptacle. Over by the exit, Kristin had stopped and texted into her phone.

She typed in a few more letters, pressed send, then directed eyes at him that were as clear blue as an Indiana summer. Was there a flicker of something there?

Therapy. *You're here to get that release from physical therapy.*

"I'd like to check in on you later, just in case, you know?"

The corners of her mouth twitched up. "I don't even know your name."

"Leo. Leo Galloway."

She blinked and looked again, twice. "Heath's best friend in high school? Remember me?"

He stepped back, frowning. "I haven't forgotten, but I didn't recognize 'Sam.'" Heath's little sister had been five years younger and looked nothing like this stunning woman.

Those luscious lips were now in a straight line. Maybe he'd thought of her as more than a friend before? "That's my middle name." She shoved her hand toward him, and he took her firm grip into his. "Kristin Sa-man-tha Barclay."

Her skin was warm and soft. "Guess I don't remember your middle name. This warrants more of a catch-up." He gestured to the nearest empty table and took a seat in the closest chair. "Can't believe we didn't recognize each other. It's been a while."

They'd all been inseparable growing up—as close as high school boys who let a baby sister tag along occasionally could be.

They stared at each other, and he broke the silence. "Heath and I lost touch. Last I heard he was in Cape Town."

Her shoulders relaxed and the crinkle in her forehead receded. She took the chair across the table from him. "Still the same Heath. I don't hear from him, either."

Word had come through his brothers that her parents had passed away, one after the other, several years back.

"I'm in no position to judge. Heath was such an old soul, like everybody said. When we were kids, he was the one who said my art was going to go places. That meant everything. I'm snapping some shots in case I want to create a painting from them."

"Yeah, he saw what the rest of us couldn't…" Her voice trailed off. "Maybe if I'd listened to him, I'd have spared myself some grief."

Her blue eyes misted over.

He swallowed a lump in his throat. "I could've been a better friend, to both of you." After art school, he'd worked on a commission in Italy for two years, his first taste of the money to be made by his talent. The work had built on what he'd done before and took him to a whole new level of accomplishment.

She rewarded him by smiling again. "I'm so proud of you. Didn't recognize you from the news pictures."

He lifted his cowboy hat and ran his fingers through the shorter hairstyle he'd gotten before coming home. "Decided the artist with flowing locks might not play so well in Fair Creek."

She studied his face. "You always had great hair. Look, I'm heading to a meeting, so I've only got a couple more minutes. But it was nice to take a break. I've been running pretty hard."

"You never stopped when I knew you. So, what's been keeping you busy?"

He'd always had a soft spot for her. His junior year when he was on break from college, she'd squeezed him into her schedule and they'd gotten ice cream, had a good time. But the big brother role lingered on. She'd still been a kid to him.

The Kristi sitting in front of him had grown into an exceptionally pretty woman, without leaving her tomboy sturdiness behind. A breath of fresh air.

She glanced at her smart watch. "I'm repurposing my grandma's old farmhouse I inherited. You were there when we were kids. All the rooms need fresh paint and maybe some murals, if I can find the right person."

He leaned forward, startled by how much he wanted to know more. At least he was interested in seeing her again, anyway.

"I'd like to help you. I'm on a bit of a hiatus from my art."

Painting on plaster to pretty-up a room had an air of utility about it. It sounded relaxing, and his counselor had told him to stop taking on intense work for a while.

She sat up in her chair. "Great. You could take all the time you need. We're just getting started, and I'm in no hurry." There was that smile, as if he'd painted the moon, how she had looked at him as a child. Maybe he'd get to see her when he came in to work, and that would be all the payment he needed.

Then she was gone, and he headed to his doctor appointment. Seeing Kristin was just what he needed. He felt lighter and more hopeful than when he'd arrived in Fair Creek earlier.

# Chapter 3

Kristin pulled open the door to the hospital's infertility support group in Meeting Room B. Had she really been caught from almost fainting by that hunk? Yeah, right before she found out he was Leo Galloway from one of the most prominent families in Fair Creek. The Galloways were everybody's business and always had been.

Her heart rate still hadn't settled from chatting with him. She hadn't spent time around any man in, well, she wasn't sure how long. That had to be why she reacted to him like that.

Wasn't it?

Being friends with Heath had given Leo a special place in her heart. Plus, she might have had a slight crush on him when they were kids.

*Get your mind on what's important, Kristin.* Motherhood.

Babies. Could that procedure Dr. Jarvis had done been successful? Tears pricked the back of her eyes and she blinked. If she was pregnant, there would be no father in the picture. As many problems as she and Craig had, she hadn't been able to deny a chance at life for her embryos. She could almost smell the baby powder.

*This must be what crazy feels like. Lord, help.*

"Hey. You okay? Almost time to start." Beth, her friend in the group, rushed toward her, thick, reddish curls flowing. They had bonded at Kristin's first support meeting upon returning to Fair Creek, and her T-shirt said, "Infertility Warrior." People from surrounding areas all came to this bigger hospital for these specialized treatments not available in small towns.

Kristin forced a smile and patted her computer bag. "Always excited to spread the word about Miracle Mommies." Going through so much had taught her the true meaning of inner strength. Nothing got her down. Not for long, anyway.

Beth waved her perfectly manicured hand, with the nails painted in a bold geometric pattern, over toward the small cluster of women sitting in the semi-circle of chairs. "They're ready to begin. Thought you were going to miss the intros for a minute there." Beth's latest cycle must have failed. She always rewarded herself for surviving the baby disappointments with a trip for a mani-pedi at Little Tootsies.

Kristin gathered Beth into a full-body hug and whispered into her ear, "You know I'd never skip out on you. Got tempted by the coffee shop is all, ran into a guy from school. Can you believe it?"

Beth pulled away and focused on Kristin's face. "Is he handsome?"

Like most people in the room, Beth had a partner in the treatments. In her case, it was her husband. Kristin kept her status mostly to herself when she was at group, except for Beth.

"I forgive you for asking. Honestly, they don't get better looking than Leo Galloway." She kept on moving into the room. "You know I'm not ready."

"So you've said."

"I'm serious."

Beth glanced at her smart watch. "But you know what they say, God's timing isn't ours. Now, hold onto that thought while I get the meeting started."

More than thirty minutes later, everyone had introduced themselves, told how far along they were in treatment, and the business meeting had ended.

The support group didn't replace an endocrinologist's care. But they learned from one another, sometimes taking questions back to their own doctors. They commiserated on drug side effects and people who didn't understand what they were going through or those who judged the treatment choices. Occasionally, a doctor or therapist spoke at the meeting.

In the good news department, someone reported a previous attendee had gotten pregnant, just like Mandi. Kristin admired and respected all of them—including the ones who were still waiting like her—and those who succeeded and were sent on their way cheerfully, mostly. They collectively kept their fingers crossed that they would each have their own miracle come true one day.

Finally, Beth introduced her to give the presentation. The technology worked, thank goodness. A beautiful photo of the outside of Granny's house appeared on the screen. An "ahh" of appreciation rose up, and she was off and running to share Miracle Mommies with its intended audience.

During the short slide presentation, she answered questions on whether insurance would pay for its offerings. No, but she was working on getting funding to keep costs low and hoped to offer scholarships. Did women need to go to Miracle Mommies solo or could they come in groups? She was setting things up so people could come with friends, or some might come hoping to find new friends once they arrived.

"As far as I'm aware, this is the first facility of its kind and we're going to see what the needs are. I'm having some bedrooms for overnight stays. I'm in talks with Wee Willy Winkie, our local bed and breakfast, in case we need more lodging."

The newest member raised her hand. "What about those of us experiencing secondary infertility, who might need childcare?"

Kristin stepped away from the podium and directed herself to the woman. "How wonderful that you're a mother and I hope you'll be able to give them a sibling. There will be a designated playroom, some child care, and just today I've hired an artist to design a mural on that wall."

Their questions and interest encouraged her. She had a lot

to accomplish to follow through on her dream. Afterward she nibbled on the desserts and chatted, answering some individual questions, then packed up her computer and scooted out. Fair Creek was an hour away and getting home and into her bed sounded good.

On the drive, she prayed over what was on her heart. She'd never wanted to be a single mother. But getting her hopes up about the embryos seemed unwise anyway, after all of the past disappointments. She arrived home restless, not sure if she would sleep. Just putting aside her thoughts and questions surrounding her unexpected reunion with Leo Galloway proved challenging.

She couldn't wait to see him again, to get the painting going. She wasn't up for dating, in her situation, but spending time with an old friend wasn't off limits.

# Chapter 4

A week had passed since Leo had seen Kristin. It seemed longer because he'd thought about her a lot, so he came here to Hit the Nail hardware, partly for something to do. But also because they had discussed paint colors back and forth on the phone and she'd gone over what she wanted and he came in and placed the order.

His coat hung folded over his arm as he shopped. This old building still had poor heat regulation and it was baking inside. A glance out of the front picture windows showed snow on the sidewalks. Not that he had a clear view, since whoever painted the nativity scene on the window had gotten carried away with a barn that took up lots of space.

He roamed over to check out the popcorn machine that hadn't been upgraded since he was a kid. It was set up next to the big solid wood desk that held a cash register. A Christmas tree off to one side had been decorated with small versions of bright-red tools. Wrenches, screwdrivers, and plyers hung from the branches, giving a festive air to the place.

"I hoped I might run into you." Kristin came up beside him, fumbling with her coat that was partway off as she walked. "Hot in here, isn't it?"

At the sound of her voice and her admission she wanted to meet up, he worked to keep a goofy grin from his face. "Let me help. Is this going on or off?"

Holding the blue puffer jacket while she worked her arm out of one sleeve, her fruity scent wafted over. "Not sure, I'm a little distracted right now. Are you coming or going?"

His heart rate kicked up speed, even more so when his fingers touched her blond, silky hair that rested on her collar as he pulled a side of her coat from off her shoulder. "I'm not staying on task myself. Coming in here brought back a lot of memories."

Above the bird seed aisle, a sprig of mistletoe attached to the ceiling caught his eye, putting his thoughts into overdrive.

He seriously needed to get a grip.

"Well, I ordered all the paint shades you texted to me you wanted right here, and the paint texture named after that TV show was on sale. They're going to mix all the colors up for me and deliver it this afternoon."

They fell into step together, heading for the door.

A glimpse of her out of the corner of his eye verified that she'd grown more beautiful. She was so gorgeous, she took his breath away. The smile she offered up dazzled him, although it didn't reach her eyes. He couldn't shake that she was dealing with something she wasn't telling him.

"Love that you shopped local, and now we've run into each other again."

A pleasant warmth filled his chest. Maybe their reconnecting had meant something to her too? Her pale complexion brought out the blue of her eyes, like pools of light, and he fought the urge to hug her to him for some reason.

"Wasn't sure if I could get everything here. But they had it all." At the door, she rested her hand on his arm. He tingled where her soft touch reached through his sleeve.

She seemed stalled, and had just stopped in front of the doors.

She looked up at him. "A walk in fresh air might help to clear my head, if you can spare the time."

"That sounds fine. Getting reacquainted with the town has been good. I'm home to Galloway Farm to relax." For how marvelously well that was working out, with time on his hands and a woman he thought about constantly who did nothing but confuse him.

The sidewalks had been cleared and a few inches of snow were piled on both sides. Each mom-and-pop business along Main Street had a green-and-cream striped awning above it.

As they walked along, they passed replicas of old-fashioned black street poles that had been decorated with green wreaths and bright-red bows. Maybe he would do some paintings of this street? The storefront windows were painted with various holiday scenes. Delaney's diner window featured colorfully dressed carolers in coats with scarves around their necks underneath a pole that shone a yellow light. The Christmas scenes gave Fair Creek the look of a small, picturesque village.

They walked the entire street, which wasn't long, then turned around and came back. His truck was parked in front of the hardware.

"Brr. I'm getting cold."

"Want to go cruising through town?"

Once they were inside his truck, he looked over at her, and she'd leaned back in the seat, sort of melting into a relaxed position, not sitting up tense or rigid. He leaned over and turned the heat vents her way. "It's neat how they've kept the stores the same. I used to love going to Hit the Nail when I was in high school."

"I know. It was a treat when you guys let me go along. They had suckers at the counter. You'd spend hours finding the right nail or screw or thingamajig."

He chuckled. "I've forgotten all about that word. That must have been a total bore for you."

"Nope. Hanging out with the big boys was what I lived for. All the girls were jealous. They thought you guys were so cute and told me about the crushes they had on you."

He pulled to a stop at Fair Creek's only traffic light in the middle of town and tilted his head toward her. "What about you?"

Were her cheeks a bit flushed?

"I'll never tell. It was a good childhood, wasn't it? So normal. I've been through a lot since then, Leo. I won't sugarcoat it. I don't think I'd have made it if I hadn't had the good start that I did."

He looked into her eyes, the sadness there giving her an almost illuminated beauty. Not that he wanted to pry, but it was important to convey that he heard her, having no idea what she was talking about. "I'm sorry to hear that. Wish I had been there for you."

"There was nothing you, not Heath, or anybody else could do."

"I'm a good listener."

The sun peeked out and shone into the truck, and she pulled the visor down, her fingers trembling slightly. "Keep on keeping on. It's what I'm all about."

What could be wrong? Maybe looking back on old, old memories wasn't such a bad thing for her. The energy coming off her was hard to read. He glimpsed a brightness in her eyes, like the beginning of tears.

"I hope you'll tell me what's bothering you, when you're ready. Sitting here like this, it's all coming back."

She nodded. "That time they had awards night, and you didn't tell anybody you were getting one. Our moms happened to be in the grocery store that afternoon, and mine spilled the beans on you when she said she'd see your mom at the awards night. Seeing you get that award was the first time I got how talented you are. Your self-portrait still hangs in the school hallway, from what I understand."

Her mom had been a schoolteacher. "Hometown crowd. Always the easiest to please. I don't honestly remember the details but sounds like something I'd do." He grinned, aware that he was laying it on thick, but he didn't care.

Was he flirting? He didn't know.

She patted his arm, and the warmth settled through to his heart. Why was he reacting to this situation this way, to her?

"I hope you're kidding. I'd be sad if you still don't get how gifted you are." An energy, or maybe a slight tremor, came through her hand as she left it on his arm, almost as if she were drawing strength from him.

What was up with her? If only she would tell him. But prying wasn't his style. He was a private person himself.

His work was a complicated subject. "Can we talk about something else?"

"Of course. I'm sorry if I made you uncomfortable. I guess I was always a little protective of you. I know the guys used to tease you for your gift, and it bothered me. Fair Creek was the typical Indiana school, more interested in sports than anything. Basketball's everything here. That why you left?"

He didn't want to go back to when he had been her age. He'd had a slight build and hadn't fit in with the other farm kids, not in interests or temperament. He still didn't know what he'd done to get punched in a hallway, to be teased and generally made miserable in middle school. Getting his growth spurt so late hadn't helped. Some people were bullies because they could be and were physically bigger. When the schools all came together and he'd met Heath in high school, things had gotten better.

"What I wanted wasn't offered around here." He'd leave it at that. Dad hadn't taken him seriously when he said he wanted to be an artist, either. Had been mad at him for wanting a different kind of life. Getting no support for what he loved still stung. What he'd been through was part of the reason he had no interest in having a family.

He didn't want to part with her, but there were only so many side streets he could take in Fair Creek, it was so small. "Where to next?"

"I'm feeling better. Why don't we go to Miracle Mommies where you'll be painting?" She pointed to a street that angled off Main, which was also toward Galloway Farm. He made the turn.

The snow scattered over the dark-brown, frozen ground and bare trees with the white stuff in the crooks made for a pretty scene. His fingers itched for his paintbrushes and a canvas. It was going to be harder than he thought to leave painting behind, even for a short time. And maybe he didn't need to, as long as he didn't get so driven about it.

But he'd never been one to go halfway on anything. The painting this image conjured in his mind now shifted right over into marketing mode. Would anyone buy it? Would it represent a new phase in his career and be more than just dabbling for relaxation? So many questions and no answers. Maybe he really did have a problem with unwinding. Thing was, that mentality of go-go-go had made him, and if he could back off and become more laid back—and he wasn't sure that he could—he didn't know that he wanted to. After this short hiatus, he secretly hoped he'd come back stronger than ever, possibly do his best work yet.

She tugged on his sleeve. "Well, that was our turn back there."

"Sorry. Guess my mind wandered." He stopped the truck and looked to see if anyone was coming either way on the deserted road. Nope, there were no vehicles coming in either direction. In the clear, he turned the truck around, which took several adjustments because the pavement wasn't that wide.

She smiled, a serene look, her expression still relaxed. "You were a million miles away. Care to share?"

He didn't. "No." Maybe it was their age difference because he wasn't one of those people who needed for everyone to know his thoughts, or even one person, for that matter. Maybe he'd been solo for too long, but it suited him fine.

Right, that was another thing his therapist said wasn't good for his mental health—so much alone time.

In his silence, she filled the gap. "I shouldn't have asked. Maybe I'm just trying to get out of my own head, away from everything on my mind."

With the truck righted and going down the correct road, he shrugged. "I get lost in my thoughts a fair amount. It's a hazard of the job—and living alone probably. Painting takes more time and focus than most people realize. I've honed my concentration skills to a science."

They came upon the big farmhouse he'd been in many times over the years and not paid much attention to. The wraparound porch always seemed inviting, but the place had looked abandoned anytime he'd seen it more recently. Now, some renewal seemed to be taking place.

Kristin's whole face brightened, and her cheeks turned pink. "Here we are. Pull into the drive and park over there by the barn."

He did as instructed. "We're neighbors. Guess I haven't thought about it in a long while." In the distance, a fence that bordered Galloway Farm showed that the properties were next to one another, but his family's buildings weren't in view. Those would be miles away.

"How many acres is this?" Now he was the one being nosy. Why did he care anyway? "If you don't mind saying, that is."

"It's fine. About 275 acres. I've had hard times, but like I told you, there's been ups and downs. Some was my personal life and finances. Well, after our parents died, Heath and I had their insurance money in a trust, and it did well. Really, really well."

He was so happy for her. "That's great."

"I mean, it's not how I ever wanted to have money, and I'd do anything to have them back, obviously. Granny's place is big and was pretty ramshackle when I took ownership. But the bones were good, and I've got plans for it. There are buildings in back, and the best one's where I live."

"You've got a nice setup. I'm impressed."

"Now let me show you the details."

# Chapter 5

Kristin worked with her computer, pretending to take a few glimpses to admire the snowy wonderland that were her fields outside the windows. But nothing compared to her view of Leo's cowboy hat tipped back just enough that she could see his handsome face. Dark, soulful eyes threw off messages she wasn't sure how to interpret. In profile, his jawline appeared cut in steel, and her heart skipped a beat.

But then, they had met six and half days ago in that coffee shop, and she'd thought about him every day since—more than once a day, if she was being honest. She'd been counting days for multiple reasons, and she wasn't quite believing anything happening.

*I don't believe Dr. Jarvis said the embryos are viable. All three of them.*

She wouldn't think about that. She hit send to print out the plans.

A scratching sound on the back door caught her attention. She went and opened it. Her dog, an all-black mix, ran in and jumped on Leo—more like tackled him. Training a dog had been last on her list.

"Bandit, get down." She reached for her dog's collar and tried to haul her from the cowboy, and noticed Leo seemed to have grown taller since their school days. The dog didn't reach his chest, not even close. And what a nice, broad chest Leo had.

Where had that come from? She hadn't been interested in any man since the terrible struggles with her ex and then his tragic death.

"Bandit!" Bandit's paws didn't budge from the man's waist. Leo petted her and her long, pink tongue lolled out. If dogs could smile, that's what she would be doing.

He rubbed Bandit's ears. "She's not bothering me."

Kristin went to a small table in the corner of the room with a printer and collected the papers. "Better be careful. She was a stray and starved for food and affection when I found her. You're her new best friend."

She inhaled a deep breath. Something about her pet snuggling up to the man was breaking down her defenses. She wondered if he felt the same. He hadn't smiled this much and looked so comfortable since they had first re-met.

Memories came back to her. "We used to run around in the fields with your dog when we were kids, didn't we? Should've known you'd be a dog guy."

"With going to locations for work, sometimes for extended periods, I haven't had a dog since we were kids." He gave the dog one more pat on the head, gently took each paw in one of his big, muscular hands, then lowered the dog's paws to the floor. "Bandit, sit." The dog sat, and Leo grinned at Kristin. "Guess I've still got it. Didn't realize how much I've missed having a dog. And I can't get over how you're all grown up. More pretty than ever. Hope I'm not making you uncomfortable."

No mistaking the sensation of heat rising in her cheeks.

She swallowed. Nothing at that moment could have pleased her more than his complimenting her. She faked a cheesy grin. "It's rough but I'll adjust."

He smiled and changed the subject. He'd always been attuned to her feelings, now that she thought about it. No wonder she had a crush on him then, and maybe still did. He reached out for the papers. "Let's see those. Can't wait to hear your plans."

Bandit went and curled up in the corner. Leo leaned in a little closer to her than he had before. At this angle, her head came about level with his shoulder. He smelled good, like coming home. If only she could brush her cheek on his broad shoulder like she almost desperately wanted to.

What was wrong with her? Three babies. Freaking out seemed the best option. *Lord, I'm going to need all the shoulders to lean on I can find.*

They went through the pages and she pointed out the details of her plans. Then they walked through the rooms, and she directed him toward which would be the community room, and bedrooms for guests. The remodeled kitchen sparkled in its shiny newness, yet her designer had preserved a hominess, using the old wooden trim that had been freshly sanded and stained. Other touches would add more coziness as the project progressed, like special lighting and the murals Leo came up with. Paint would make a huge difference and Leo had helped select paint colors to create the mood she wanted in the various rooms.

The tour over, she stepped back into the community room, and he followed. "I'll bet these windows draw in a lot of sun, when the sun is out."

The room had been constructed when big old windows were the norm. "They do, and those are new and supposed to be the latest in keeping in heat."

"Seems like you've thought of everything."

"Did our best."

She needed to go to the restroom and was feeling urgent about it. What had she been thinking to bring him here? By catching a ride, she owed him some explanation. Her situation was going to get out into the world sooner than later. He was a family friend, and she didn't know why she felt so hesitant to tell him, for anyone to know. But those who were aware of her situation would want an update. There'd be so many questions. She had no answers.

He walked around the room and spread his hand out, letting his fingers run along some of the drywall. "I guess I pictured rough walls, like the typical old farmhouses would have. But this is smooth and will go on nicely. It's a perfect canvas really."

She exhaled. Oh, right. Focus on the paint. "I'm glad you think so. I feel really strange having an artist of your caliber do random work that could be contracted out. In the playroom, I envision a mural of a hill with cows and horses and barns, if you agree. Are you sure about this? Guess I got carried away by seeing you again, and it sounded fun to work on something together."

He came over to her. "You always had good instincts. You have no idea how much I'm looking forward to this."

Those eyes. He might be taller and more filled out, a man, no longer any traces of the boy he'd been, but those pools of brown? She fell right into them as she always had.

"That's all I needed to hear. Let's sit and decide where we go from here. Figure out a schedule."

His face was so close to hers. Her heart skipped a bit under his gaze. When he spoke, his voice sounded even deeper. "I like that idea."

A shiver went up her spine. She held up a finger in between them. "I'm sorry, the sofa in what we call the sunroom is the only furniture. Let me make a pitstop." She made a half-turn toward the hallway to the bathroom. "Why don't you go have a seat? When I'm back, we'll see what's in the fridge."

"A refrigerator and no kitchen table?"

"Have you forgotten my love of food? Any place I'm going to spend time will have sustenance." She giggled, which didn't help her bathroom needs.

His eyes didn't leave hers. "A woman after my own heart. See you in a few."

She power walked away, reached the big bathroom in seconds, and once done with her business, rinsed her hands. Her face in the mirror seemed a little more rounded, a little flushed maybe. Pregnancy signs?

Surely, it was her imagination because it was much too soon. Wasn't it? What was that popular book her friends had read on this subject about what to expect? She'd speed up her next book order and add that one.

One thing was for sure. She had no idea what to expect next from Leo Galloway. As she rinsed off her hands, a shiver ran through her. She could hardly wait to find out.

# Chapter 6

Leo yawned as he drove up the long lane to his family's farm. He hadn't slept well last night after leaving Kristin's. Seeing her again had stirred up old memories and new feelings. They'd spent the afternoon together and after Hit the Nail delivered the paint, they got everything ready to start. Vast fields spread out in every direction. He inhaled, putting thoughts of Kristin out of his mind.

Not that he really could.

Once past the tall wooden arch over the entrance with the shiny new lettering saying Galloway Sons Farm, Leo noted the barns were basically the same. Dad had been gone a year next month. About the only thing he and his brothers had agreed on was to insert the word "sons" into the name of the farm, as a tribute to Dad. Come to think of it, he had expressed mixed emotions about that but had been outvoted.

He slowed down as he came toward the main house. There were some additional buildings sprinkled in, but the main configuration remained, etched in his memory for all time. His Dad had not been the father he wanted—a man who worked the land hard for his family but couldn't give encouragement to a son going into the arts.

Something in his chest resonated with the place though, catching him completely by surprise. Growing up here is what had made him, the beginning of how he saw the world. A black-and-white dog bounded out from nowhere.

Leo opened the truck door, and the dog came over and sniffed him. He patted its head, the fur surprisingly wispy for how thick it looked.

"How are you doing?" The dog leaned down on its haunches and then flopped on the ground for a belly rub. Leo stroked the fur on the dog's stomach.

An art piece featuring all these barns formed in his mind. It had been so long since he painted anything here—decades.

What was going on with him? He'd never thought of any of this in an artistic way, not since he was a kid. He'd gone through art school in Rhode Island. Afterward, he ignored what he'd always known, these familiar surroundings, thinking they were invalidated for some reason. He'd never given it significance before. Maybe if he'd had better memories, that would have helped.

"You going to stay out there with the dog forever? Didn't

figure you for a wimp." Caleb's voice hadn't changed at all, not since it had gone deeper when he was fourteen and Leo had been twenty-four. They'd all made fun of him when it had broken at times in the transition. A warmth formed in his chest.

"Don't give me a hard time." His voice was thick with emotion. This was why he'd gotten a hotel rather than coming out to the farm. He'd landed in his private plane on the family airstrip in back of the property and headed to his lodging in town.

Maybe he was going soft that he had come at all. Coming back here might not have been his best idea, or his therapist's. Not that he really had a choice, with Dad's will's stipulation.

*Lord, why am I here? These memories aren't what I anticipated, and I'm not sure I like this.*

Leo glanced in the truck and decided he didn't need to get anything out of it for now. He walked toward the front porch where Caleb stood. "Cabs, I always thought animals were friendlier than people. You've just proved the point. Got a better greeting from your pup."

His brother stepped off the porch and met him halfway, giving him a bear hug. They held on for just a couple of seconds. How could this full-grown man be his little brother?

His brother spoke next to his ear. "Mom taught us manners, but they never took with me."

He laughed and Caleb joined him, easing the tension. "You seem like you've done all right, if the reports I hear on your construction empire are anything close to accurate." Caleb had made a name for himself in construction. All the Galloway sons had made their mark in some way.

They started walking into the house together. "I wasn't expecting you today."

"Got things squared away and was able to come a bit sooner. When your therapist tells you to take a break or there's going to be a struggle—"

"Great to see you."

Oh, right, these folks didn't talk openly about therapists. Probably needed it most of all.

But it really was fantastic to see his brother. He and Caleb had always gotten along well. Neither was much for keeping up with phone calls or communication, but the tension in his shoulders loosened. They were good.

"Wish we would have some alone time, but I've got a full house today."

What did that mean? Caleb was still the single man he'd always been, wasn't he? "What, you have a party last night or something? On a weeknight?" In his younger days, he would fill up the house with a party, and Mom put Leo in charge of clearing people out. She liked to look like the good guy.

Caleb glanced over at him. "No, I left that behind so long ago, can't remember exactly when. Thought we sent you a Christmas card. Or Annie did anyway."

"That would involve being in the same place enough to get the mail. So, sorry about that, if there was an important message I've missed."

They reached the porch, and Caleb opened the door to move

inside. "No worries. You're going to get caught up. Real quick."

Sounds of laughter and squeals of young children came from the dining room. They came into the kitchen first. It looked like a cyclone had hit and thrown baby things on every surface. All the counters were covered up. Bags with their zippers open showed diapers. Cups with little spouts on the end were tumbled into a pile, and opened mini cereal boxes were piled on the side. Small bowls were randomly stacked, and some milk dribbled onto the counter.

Coming farther into the room, Leo chose where to step carefully, missing little books with thick pages that had been tossed on the kitchen floor, along with a toy barn and horses and the little plastic farmer, all spread around in no particular order, most of them on their side or upside down.

A woman with blond hair came through the entryway from the dining room, a very young boy on one hip, with his shirt stained with something dark that looked sticky.

"Oh, I thought you were going to be gone all day! You must be Leo." She pecked Caleb's cheek, then her gaze whisked over to Leo, and a slight pink shade fell on her pale cheeks. Darting around the room, she grabbed miscellaneous items and stuffed them in bags. She hurried to the counter and picked up the cereal boxes and carried them to the trash can.

Caleb went to her and kissed her on the lips, then gave the boy a peck, too. "How you doing, buddy? Annie, don't worry about these things. You've had a lot on your plate, literally."

"We had pancakes, and more syrup ended up on his shirt

than in his mouth." Caleb caught her hand in his and pulled her over. "Annie, take a moment with my older brother, Leo, the famous artist."

Her frown disappeared, replaced by one of the most engaging smiles he'd seen, which transformed her face. She offered her hand. "Leo, I've heard you're an incredible artist and saw your work in the hallway. Just as significantly, you're the man who kept all the Galloway brothers in line growing up. I'm in awe."

Warmth filled him unexpectedly. His brothers had told this young woman more than his name? The idea pleased him more than it should have.

Caleb said, "She was behind us in school. That rock is her engagement ring. Oh, boy, I wish you were more prepared for what I'm telling you. Read your mail from now on, okay? This little guy is Drew, your nephew. He's Kayla's son, and we've borrowed him and his twin sister for a while."

That didn't sound good about Kayla's kids. Leo patted the boy's back, not sure of what to say.

It'd been so long since he'd been here, and even longer since they'd grown up together. He spoke to Annie. "Don't believe everything they've told you. I never did half what they thought. Our mother had her hands full, and maybe I helped her out a little, but that was it."

Caleb stepped over and chuffed him on the shoulder. "You were always the modest one. That is, unless you were making your drawings that landed everywhere. You're the reason we had a humongous refrigerator, more space to post things on, and every sink paint-stained. When you left for art school, we missed your sketches as much as we did you."

He couldn't help smiling. "At least I didn't leave Legos underfoot, Cabs. I'm lucky I can walk. One night, a plastic chunk was so embedded in my heel, I considered a trip to the E.R."

Annie had gone to the sink, held a paper towel under the water, and mopped at the sticky shirt. After a moment, she said to Drew, "I give up. Let's go find something else for you to wear." They left the room with one of the bags.

Guess his brother wasn't done with him yet though. "You've always been prone to exaggeration. Besides, Legos were the early beginnings of my brilliant career in construction."

"Oh, talk about stretching the truth. You make it sound like you grew up to build the next Empire State Building."

Another woman, this time a striking redhead, came into the room with a boy on one hip and a girl on the other. Pinks and blues must have been a way they told them apart? Every one of the young ones looked similar in coloring and features.

To his single lifestyle, they were a jolt to his system. "How many people are you housing here, Cabs?"

"Very funny. If you read mail, kept an updated email like normal people, you wouldn't be standing there with your mouth open."

He pressed his lips together and held his tongue. No point in explaining again how he obsessed about his work, went months without coming up for air, if then. Hated computers. The list went on. Pointless to get defensive. "I'm here now. Please fill me in."

"This is Sierra, who's about to join the family. Wyatt put a ring on it last Fourth of July.

Max is Wyatt's little boy. Ella and Drew are twins."

Annie had magically popped a clean shirt on Drew and corralled an older girl who just stepped in over toward Leo. "Chloe, say hi to Leo. He's Caleb's brother, so he's another Galloway who will be your uncle soon."

His head spun with all this, not sure he could keep them straight in his mind, but the formerly quiet child's face broke out in a big smile. She seemed to come alive as she offered her hand to shake. "I'm so lucky to have you for an uncle. This is such a fun family. My mommy is an only child, and now I'm getting so many uncles. Nice to meet you, Leo!"

Her tiny, warm hand melted his heart. "The pleasure is all mine, honey. Caleb always did have good people skills, and I can see you'll be an upgrade to the family. Welcome!" He let go of her hand, unprepared for how she touched his heart. Maybe he'd missed out on something by embracing his bachelor ways?

Nah, he'd been doing great with his choices.

Hadn't he? But there was something nice about not being judged for anything, for being accepted just as he was, even if by an innocent kid.

He found himself grinning at the child, who continued to look at him like she'd won a prize just by meeting him. He would definitely need to up his game in the uncle department. She made him want to.

His head spun. Where was Kayla? He might be out of it, but

he had never heard of kids not being with their parents, unless they were on vacation. Sure, it happened, but not to any Galloway he'd ever known. That counted all of his many cousins.

Caleb came over, the biggest grin on his face. "I can see you're overwhelmed. Might as well get all the news out. Assuming you didn't get the wedding invitations either? Caleb and I will be having a double wedding come Christmas Eve. The barn's just about ready, and I'll show you when you're ready."

Not even pretending to keep it together, Leo pulled over a chair from the table in the corner and sat. Hadn't his brothers been just kids the last time he looked? Weddings weren't his thing. Now he had to psych himself up for two at the same time. He sent up a prayer for strength.

# Chapter 7

ristin lay in her bed and willed her limbs to move. The sun shone through the lace curtains Granny had hung when she was a little girl, making patterns on the walls. She'd slept more in these past two days than in her entire life. Letting her body rest through the physical and mental impact she was going through seemed like a good idea. From her position flat on her back, she lifted her arms overhead and stretched, letting out a moan.

Bandit nudged the bedroom door open and came in, her tail curved upward, with it gently waving and swishing as she made her way over to the bed. The dog sat, and her gaze was at eye level with Kristin's head on her pillow.

Lowering her arms, she hugged herself to complete her stretch, then stroked the top of Bandit's head. Ever since she had parted with Leo the night before last, she'd been exhausted. Getting the news that she was expecting triplets had no doubt been part of it. But not sharing her news with her big brother's best friend had taken more control than she'd dreamed possible.

She'd been contending with her predicament or whatever she'd call it, but he had not seemed totally at ease himself. Plus, what kind of insanity was it to have a world-renowned painter work on her old farmhouse's renovation? What was she thinking?

She stopped petting Bandit, grabbed the pillow from the other side of the bed and hugged it close. He'd told her to call him when she wanted to come by and see the farm again. What was that supposed to mean? Of course, she wouldn't. He was probably just being polite, didn't know how to end the evening after talking about paint colors.

In one-and-a-half weeks, she'd have her ultrasound and they'd detect the fetal heartbeats. *Thank you, Lord.* What was it that people said? Feed your faith and starve your fear.

A cold, wet nose pressed onto her hand. She resumed petting the dog. "You want to help me, girl?"

The brown eyes bore into hers. "You do, don't you?"

She continued to pet her dog, and Bandit moved her head to have her ears scratched. "Or maybe you want food?"

She'd left food out in the dog bowl like normal, hadn't she? She must have. So many things she did regularly were just habit.

The Lord knew she would have three babies to feed, and how was that going to go? She could barely care for a dog. Her heart beat a little faster and she tried not to overreact.

Bandit continued to stare her down.

"How did this happen?"

Maybe sorting things out, going over how she'd gotten to this place, would help. Getting up and actually moving might be an idea, but she was bone weary.

"Everything was great in school. I excelled at whatever I tried. To be fair, if I tried something I wasn't good at, I didn't continue with it."

Her heart rate had leveled out. The tension in her shoulders lessened. Maybe this was a form of talk therapy. She sat up. Bandit's eyes opened a little wider, like she was hopeful. "Hey, want me to get you some fresh water, check your bowl while we talk?"

She pulled on some fuzzy socks she kept by the bed. Grabbed a robe. The house was cold in the winter. Bandit's tail took up wagging vigorously now. Good thing she'd put away all of Granny's fragile glass items when Bandit moved in, or that tail might have caused some damage on anything sitting on the lower tables. They went into the hallway together.

The dog stayed outside a lot, which was how she'd met Leo at Miracle Mommies, just roaming the property on her own. Once she'd found out Kristin was over there quite a bit, she'd experimented with scratching on the door to be let in.

Here at home, Kristin kept cloths and items to rinse off Bandit's feet by the back door, for anytime she was coming in, and whenever she brought her in for the night.

They walked through Granny's big, sunny kitchen, careful to

avoid the sharp corners of the butcher block table. She patted Bandit's head. "I keep you in at night, don't I? Because we have coyotes and all kind of animals out here."

They arrived in the mud room where everything dog related stayed. "Oh, you were out of food. Mommy's sorry." She opened up the bag of dog food from where she kept it on the shelf and scooped out two heaping scoops and dropped them into the bowl.

Bandit sat until both scoopfuls of dog food were in the dish. And still she waited. "Somebody trained you, girl, didn't they?"

The dog sat at attention, eyes on Kristin, waiting for the cue word. When she'd first adopted the dog after noticing it roaming the fields for a bit, losing weight, she had looked up some basic dog training techniques on the internet.

"Go ahead."

Bandit dug into the food. She'd never been able to get her to eat neatly like the dog whisperers taught on T.V.

In less than two minutes, the dog's eating slowed. Maybe she was full or had gotten the edge of her hunger quenched. She paused and lapped up water from her water dispenser, which didn't need refilled.

As her dog ate, she felt so much better, she kept talking. "Anyway, everything was perfect when I was in school, maybe a little too perfect. Craig was the football quarterback, and I was head cheerleader, two years apart in school. He worked at a Fair Creek financial office, asked me out senior year, and after I graduated, we dated another year. Marriage was the natural next step."

The dog finished eating and sat next to her, seeming to enjoy the sound of her voice. Maybe they'd both been lonely. Kristin retraced her steps back through the house, and the dog followed. "Things fell apart when Craig's job transferred him to Toledo. We were away from family. I had a job at a bank and was getting promotions, but we wanted to start our family."

Back in her bedroom, Kristin eyed with longing the dip in her pillow where her head had been.

She flopped back on the bed. Living alone had its advantages. She eyed Bandit. "Don't judge. The fairy tale crashed, couldn't have a baby, Craig got addicted to pain pills, nothing I tried worked."

Her eyes fluttered shut.

A phone rang, and Leo's name went across her screen. She answered, and after greeting her, he dove right in.

"You weren't thinking of leaving my offer on the table, were you? Can you come out and see the farm? I know you love animals. That I remember. "

Kristin cuddled her pillow and smiled into the receiver. Maybe she hadn't been tired, but discouraged? "I'm glad you called."

"I'll warn you. I have something to ask you."

The familiar knot in her gut started to form. *Don't be silly. There's no way he knows you're pregnant.*"

"Now I'm intrigued. I've got something on my mind, too. Let me handle things here and I'll head over." *Like brushing my teeth and finding clothes to wear. Then dropping a baby bombshell.*

Kristin lounged in bed one more minute, counting one Mississippi, two Mississippi, and so on until she made it to sixty. On the last number, she threw off the covers and headed to her dresser for clothes.

On the way, a white, long-sleeved T-shirt she tossed over a vintage upholstered chair looked comfortable. Granny's furniture had been expensive when she purchased it years ago. Now, it was classic, and the cabinets with her dishes comforted Kristin. She'd thought of replacing things with something modern, but these made her feel loved, like Granny was still around. Two years had gone by quickly. It had taken eighteen months to get the property exchange squared away. She tugged on the jeans from the nearby ottoman, snatched up the T-shirt and put it on along with her jean jacket. A check in the full-length mirror mounted on the wall brought a frown. Too ordinary. She needed pizazz.

She would take her time and get the look she wanted. Meeting with him shouldn't have this much significance. But she wasn't going to analyze it.

She didn't get out enough, obviously. This would be fun. Stripping off her top as she went, she opened the closet door and ran her fingers along the row of hangers until she reached the red retro snap-styled cowgirl shirt she'd bought on a whim.

Slipping it on felt right, and one glance in the mirror confirmed that it played up her blond hair. She exuded confidence and smiled back at herself with attitude. Perfect. Light makeup and heavy mascara did the trick to brighten her coloring.

A cold bottle of water from the fridge, the last brown-sugar pop tart, and she was ready. In the coat closet, she clawed through footwear on the floor until she located her well-worn, tan cowboy boots.

Some days, she felt like she was run as ragged as her favorite boots. *Lord, lift me up.*

She shoved her feet in while she reached around on the top shelf above her head for her black cowboy hat with metal squares down near the rim. Her keys stayed in her leather, stitched clutch, which she grabbed. At the door, the canvas bag filled with her new crochet project reminded her she was supposed to relax through the day. Picking it up, she let Bandit out as she went. A barn with a doggie door was there if she needed shelter.

Her little burnt-orange Chevy truck, Beanie, waited near the water pump by the shed. The chill made her eyes sting. Her breath puffed out little clouds in the air. Coats didn't appeal to her, and she wouldn't be out long.

But one never knew what plans a cowboy might come up with. She let out a groan and turned back to the house. She bit into the icing, then pastry, and finally sank into the brown sugar.

Several minutes later, now wearing her camel, lined bomber jacket, she strapped into the driver's seat and shot out of the lane heading to Galloway Sons Farm.

She turned on her playlist, then stopped the music. Too many thoughts played over and over in her mind.

And just as importantly, what could Leo Galloway have to ask her?

# Chapter 8

Leo stood on the porch that extended deep into the yard of the Galloway homestead and looked out over the fields. The coffee in his canteen warmed his hands, his only defense against the deep chill in the air.

Either this coat wasn't warm enough or he'd gotten old and spoiled. Maybe both. Getting out of Boston during the coldest months had become a habit. His place in Palm Beach had become his sanctuary.

He didn't know what had possessed him to invite Kristin. She should be here by now. Maybe she wasn't coming after all.

"This where the line for the lovelorn is forming?" Caleb let the screen door slam shut behind him as he came and stood next to Leo.

These kinds of remarks were what kept him away from this

place. Who needed it? Anyone could see he was happy on his own—mostly. "Be a pretty short line, from the looks of things."

"Not sure you've been around enough to make that kind of call."

Leo couldn't resist making a dig. Caleb had started it. "Doesn't take long to see when the hens have pecked their way in."

Caleb walked to the edge of the porch and stepped down. "Don't knock what it's like to be with a good woman 'til you've tried it. I'm not the one standing in the bitter cold looking down the lane with puppy dog eyes." He gestured for Leo to follow him out to the barn.

Caleb had read him all wrong. He just wanted to be sure Kristin was all right, like any friend would. Who was he kidding?

They walked the rest of the way in companiable silence, until Caleb turned the knob on the barn's side door and they both went inside. The huge building had more tractors than the last time he'd been home. Why had his brother brought him in here? Pretty sure he'd forgotten how to run farm machinery.

One look at Caleb carrying the ladder to where Mom's huge Christmas wreath hung on the wall gave the explanation. "Help me with this, would you?"

The two of them wrestled the human-sized wreath to the ground, and Leo took it from Caleb, careful not to mash the gigantic red bow. The barn was covered in fresh red paint, from the looks of it. The classically styled wreath would be the perfect complement. His brother opened the main barn door to get out the big boss truck. He positioned the ladder in its bed and used a long metal pole with a hook on the end to catch the wreath's loop. Caleb took three tries to maneuver the wreath into place on the nail Dad had put up near the barn's peak decades earlier, for this very purpose.

"Hi!"

Leo turned to see Kristin walking toward them. His heart skipped a beat, if that was possible. "There you are. You remember Caleb?" Leo climbed down out of the truck.

"I do, but it's been a long while. Took a bit more to get ready than I anticipated. Wow, that's splendid."

Caleb gave her a nod. "It's not Christmas on the farm without Mom's wreath."

She put her gloved hands together in two quick claps. "We had the best mothers ever, didn't we? I just love family traditions."

Caleb paused, then began putting away the ladder. "Glad you could be here for the annual raising of the Galloway wreath."

Leo's plans to play it cool drifted into thin air. He leaned in toward her for a hug, and she met him in the middle. Their heavy coats got in the way somewhat. Only she'd left her brown coat unbuttoned, with a red flash of material showing out from underneath, and with his coat open from when he exerted himself with the wreath, the warmth from her solid body seeped through to his chest. His heart raced, and he inhaled her fruity, clean scent, wondering if she could tell the effect she was having on him. Their embrace lasted slightly longer than necessary, since he wanted to stave off the chill for her.

*Yeah, right.*

He stepped back, a bit tongue-tied. "You could be part of the Christmas decor yourself."

She beamed and opened her coat wide, giving him the full impact of her top's Western styling. "Like my new shirt?"

He nodded, trying to form words. Her blue eyes sparkled under her dark cowboy hat. She'd loved all things cowboys as a little girl. How could he have forgotten? The pant legs of her dark jeans were tucked into her leather cowboy boots, combining their ruggedness with the glamorous red blouse, like on a fashion magazine cover.

"If you were a Christmas ornament, you'd be the brightest one on the tree."

That was true in more ways than one. He wanted to bring her home with him, right then and there.

"Well, guess I'll see you around, kids." Caleb had magically taken care of putting things back where they belonged.

Kristin's eyes widened before she tore her gaze from Leo and focused over his shoulder. "It was nice seeing you again, Caleb."

Something like a grunt came from his brother, midway on his trek back to the house. "Don't freeze out here, you two."

Leo stepped over and held out his elbow to her. For some reason, the cold wasn't bothering him anymore. "Would you like to walk around? I've got something to show you."

She latched on and managed to match him stride for stride as he guided them to the shed. It felt so right.

But what was he doing? His hermit ways lately had made him susceptible to over-the-top feelings, apparently. *You're reconnecting with an old friend, nothing more.*

Leo pulled his hand away as they approached the door.

She looked up into his face, eyes sparkling. "Your leading me to some discovery you've made brings back memories. Just being here again does. I used to love it when you and Heath were assigned as my babysitters, since it was more like being let free from Mom's watchful eye."

This was more like it. Thinking about old times. There was no future ahead for them. "You really were the busiest kid ever. The few times Heath and I were in charge of you didn't go so well."

"That's an understatement." She laughed and so did he. "Not really. It wasn't as bad as you're making it sound. Wait." She stopped. "This is the shed…"

"I don't know how you ended up on the roof that time."

"Well, it's a little shed and has a really low roof." She laughed, and he couldn't get enough of the sound. "Besides, you two knew I loved to climb."

He looked up at the roof. "It isn't *that* low. You could always use words to talk around us. Somehow, you would have blamed us for it, if anyone found out."

"What can I say? You *were* always watching superheroes in capes jumping off buildings."

He shook his head. "Keeping what happened a secret from our moms seemed like the right thing to do. No one was hurt, although Heath about had a heart attack when we found you up there."

She giggled, and he couldn't help joining in. She went into

a full-on cackle that lasted so long her eyes watered, and she gulped in air. "It feels so good to laugh. I haven't thought of any of this in forever." Too soon, the sadness flitted through her eyes, what he'd seen when he first met her at the coffee shop. "It's like, I somehow lost my way. I lost myself."

"That hurts me to hear."

Could he somehow be a part of what helped her find herself again? he wondered. If he could, he wanted to be. "Let me show you something I know you would have loved, before anyway."

He reached out his hand, and she slipped her fingers into his. Even their gloves didn't wipe out their connection. He prayed nothing would ever put another gap in their friendship.

Once he'd twisted the handle, the door swung open, and tiny sounds came from the far corner. A mustiness of sawdust and fresh-cut wood filled his senses. Tools hung on the walls, saws, and water hoses, and some he'd forgotten existed or what their names were. How many times had he spent looking for a piece of sandpaper or the right nail, wiping greasy fingers on a stained cloth. What had happened to his overalls and cap? He wanted to see them again. Needed it. He might have left, but these experiences were in him still.

A cry of joy brought him to the present. "Oh, they're adorable!" He went to where she was hunkered down looking at a mother cat and six kittens, nestled in a bed of straw on the floor.

He smiled as he knelt to be on their level. "Had a feeling you'd react this way."

She didn't make eye contact with Leo, just gazed at the black cat with white markings and her babies, all tiny variations of her. "Can I hold one?"

"Yes, for a little bit. I figured you'd want to, and since Caleb's been keeping a close eye on them, he knows how old they are and how they're doing."

She picked up a tiny black one with gray markings on its ears and looked up. "Remember that batch of kitties you guys had when we were kids?"

"Sure do. Once I got the word they were ready for visitors, I had to call. Sorry if I rushed you. You were going through something, and I know I should have waited. Only, something in me just couldn't."

# Chapter 9

"You did the right thing." Kristin thanked Leo as they stood in the barn, looking at the little animal family. Hopefully, he could see how much it meant to her to be with the kittens. "I needed this today. Whether it was your instincts or God giving you a nudge. Or both. Thank you."

"They're really special, aren't they? Something about nature puts things in perspective for me."

She nodded her head, feeling a depth of emotion that seemed out of proportion to this experience. She held back tears as she gently stroked her fingers on the tiny, furry head of the kitten in her palm. The mama watched her with a wary eye. Six kittens, all of them helpless and dependent on her for everything.

So now she was over identifying with a cat. What was wrong with her? *Lord, don't let me cry in front of Leo.* There was no reason for him to feel bad he'd brought her here. She couldn't sort out how she felt. Being near tears wasn't due to sadness exactly. The mama cat was performing the role she'd been given. In a way, Kristin was doing the same thing.

She placed a kitten back with its mother. "Between the two of us, we've nurtured them all for a few minutes. I better be getting home. I've got chores." She swallowed, still struggling.

"I can understand you've got plenty to do." He shrugged. "I'd like for you to stay, for a little longer, if you can."

"Well, I don't know…"

No truer words had been spoken. She had no idea, about anything. What was she going to do?

He stood, dusted off the knees of his pants. "Let me show you something in the house first."

Leo was being such a good friend. Could he want more? Did she? "Of course. I'm not in that much of a hurry."

Parting with him made her afraid the dam would burst on her feelings. Being with him was risky, too. Her secret weighed her down and this was only the beginning. Nine months would be forever. Soon, everyone would know. It was one thing to share her decision to save her family with close friends, another to walk down the street and have everyone see. Waddle might be the more accurate term.

Why did it matter what people thought? She'd acted out of strong convictions.

Nothing seemed easy now, and she was barely holding herself together. Could he see her lips quiver? This was so unlike her.

He walked through the building, and she followed. After he secured the door, they walked toward the house. The pressure would kill her. If not now, when?

"The reason seeing the kittens was good for me goes beyond a fun thing to do. It was more than feeling closer to God by being around nature."

He stopped and so did she. His face under his hat showed concern, his mouth in a straight line and his jaw tense. "You seemed shook up by it. But what can you tell me about what's bothering you?"

She held both hands palm up, and when they didn't shake, she breathed out a sigh.

"I'm pregnant."

The lines around his eyes deepened. Through his clenched jaw and facial expressions, she could see what she thought were a range of emotions. Fear. Disappointment maybe. "How? You said you're divorced. If you're dating someone…"

This was worse than she'd thought. But how could he possibly know the predicament she was in? "It's not what you think."

"I don't have an opinion. I thought you'd tell me what was going on. Not that you had to. It's really none of my business. This just isn't what I expected."

"I've never been in this situation before. I'm going to tell you everything, so you'll understand. I hoped you'd support me. I've tried to prepare those I'm closest to. People will talk, and it'd help if someone knows the truth. It's important to me that *you* know."

His expression full of concern, he took her hand in his. She leaned in, and they moved ahead, shoulder to shoulder.

They reached the house. He opened the door and ushered her forward. "Please, go inside."

She couldn't feel her fingertips from the cold, just in the distance from the shed to the house. Without hesitation, she went inside, and he followed. In the empty kitchen, they removed their coats and placed them over chairs.

He offered her something to drink, but she was numb. They took seats at the table. "Before you continue, I want to show you this."

He picked up something from the counter and pressed it into her hand. A lightweight keychain with a trinket shaped like a cowboy boot with the #1 painted on it lay in her palm.

"Look familiar?"

"It's from the school Santa Shop. I bought it for you one year. Can't believe you still have it."

He studied her. "I don't know why you'd think I would get rid of it." He took her hand again, the dark-cocoa shade of his eyes focused on her. "Now, tell me what's going on."

Still holding the boot, she briefed him about marrying Craig Young and their inability to have a family. His minor, unrelated surgery had been botched, and he became addicted to opioids prescribed for the pain. No rehab had worked, and divorce was the only way.

"He passed away three years ago. The bill to store our leftover embryos for the year came due. They'd been stored for more than a decade, and I called about my options. They could be discarded, or I could give them to another couple, but it would be like an adoption, going through legal steps, and I could choose a couple. Some people give theirs to science. I'm thirty-three. They're my family." She choked on the last word. "I'm giving them a chance."

"I can't honestly see how you got into this situation."

She hung onto the boot and arranged her hands in her lap. "The doctors never know what will happen with frozen embryos, and I only wanted to go through the procedure once, not go through a separate procedure for each one. What were the odds that one would take? Let alone two or three, when none of the others had? The doctor understood and left it up to me. I just felt so strongly they deserved a chance. I've put them in God's hands."

Leo couldn't let her face this alone. He went and wrapped his arms around her shoulders. "You made a brave decision. I couldn't have done it." He returned to his chair.

"The medical part wasn't easy. But no matter what some people say, the doctors don't make babies. They are miracles from God just like all babies are."

"I've never thought about any of this. Having kids isn't in my plans at all—didn't have the desire. Pretty sure I don't have what it takes to be a good father."

She studied him, his dark-brown eyes telling stories as she looked deeply. "You're such a good guy, Leo. Dads are regular people. Ever since we were kids, I knew I was safe with you. Probably the fact that you've examined yourself and think you've come up short is more than most people do, and evidence you'd make an amazing father. I mean, if you wanted to, and this isn't about you anyway."

Why had she said that? It wasn't her job to convince him of anything. Not her job to talk him into it. Nope. Not for the babies she carried or for any he might have.

She'd spent so much time thinking about babies, why some who weren't good to them had them so easily. She had to tell him, needed to tell someone. "Most people take their ability to have babies for granted. They assume they'll be able to have kids whenever they decide to. But when I went through what we did, I saw God has his hand in everything. Instead of questioning my faith, mine was strengthened. When things go wrong, you realize what a miracle every part of creation is, you know?"

Ella and Drew burst in from another room, whooping like banshees, with Annie running along behind. "Sorry for the noise," Annie said. "You looked like you were in a serious conversation there. I'm keeping them busy because it's too cold to play outside. We'll just move on through."

Kristin stood. "No need. We were wrapping things up. What's your puppy's name?"

"Scooter!" The little boy mangled the name, sounding like "shooter" but she figured it out.

"We're watching it for a friend. It's not ours," Annie said.

"Great name, anyway," she said to Drew.

He smiled and hugged the dog, which was surprisingly calm about it, except his little eyes might have pleaded for mercy.

She leaned back in the chair, relieved the heavy conversation had ended. Would Leo interact with a nearly two-year-old? The little ones peered over at him. They had on similar outfits that looked like tiny athletic wear, only one had a horse on the chest and the little girl had an image of a cartoon character, and her hair was up in tiny pigtails.

Leo bent down to their level. "Hey, it's good to see you. Give me five."

Drew let go of the dog. Leo lifted his large hand that dwarfed each one of theirs and clapped each little hand on his, one after the other.

"Now, better do what Annie says so I can finish talking to my friend, okay? Then I'll come in and pretend I'm a pony so you can ride around."

Kristin's heart melted. They nodded their heads enthusiastically and ran out of the room.

"Sorry again." Annie hurried after them.

Kristin loved that there was so much affection in this family. She regretted what she'd shared with Leo and was filled with doubt about her decision.

Leo was smiling when he turned back to Kristin. "So, what's next for you in all of this?"

Maybe it was going to be okay. She already felt a little lighter. "An appointment for an ultrasound that takes images, kind of like a video, so the doctor can see how they're doing."

"How about if I go with you?"

Kristin couldn't believe what she was hearing. Leo was offering to fulfill her greatest wish. He might seem like an unusual choice, but this was a unique circumstance, and she trusted him not to make things harder than they already were.

"You've been really wonderful about all this. I must have done something right to have a friend like you."

"I sometimes wonder if we could be more."

# Chapter 10

Leo left Kristin sitting at the table and went over to the kitchen window of Galloway Sons Farm and tried to gather his scattered thoughts. So much for relaxing at home. This place was a pressure cooker. These beautiful kids he'd met here, all of them related to him, had saved him by running in and interrupting their conversation. The intensity and subject of the conversation had nearly broken him.

She'd challenged everything he thought he believed. About himself. About her. Possibly even about God. She thought she was following his will. But three babies? He was concerned for her situation, for her health. But he didn't feel a pull to get overly involved with her babies.

Like God whispering in his ear, the questions came. What if he really was supposed to do more than his art? Had he been the selfish one, keeping himself walled off?

*Don't be ridiculous. You couldn't even keep the cultures in yogurt alive, if they needed nurtured*

Why did he feel such attraction to her if they were meant to stay in the friend zone?

Going to the ultrasound wouldn't be a big deal. It was the least he could do, and he was pretty sure Heath would have, if he'd been around.

"Scooter!" His nephew and niece ran through again.

"Kids!" Annie raised her voice this time, and the three of them ran back out.

There was a knock on the door. He didn't live here. Kristin shrugged her shoulders. He must be the designated doorman.

He opened the door. Standing on the porch, a familiar face, yet one that had aged more than he would have anticipated, greeted him. "Kayla. Come in."

The force of his little sister's hug would have toppled a smaller man. Her tight grip squeezed the air from his lungs. Leo found his voice, just barely. "You're a sight for sore eyes, you know that?" He felt her head bob up and down, nudging into his abdomen. She'd always been the shortest of their clan.

"I came to talk to Caleb."

"I'm sorry. He's not here, but he's expected shortly. Can I be of help?"

They just stood there, and she looked up so they were face to face. You could have heard the softest-bristled paintbrush drop, the room was so quiet.

Kayla's fingers loosened from his shirt, and she pulled back. With the sparkle of tears pooled in her brown eyes, the pain of all she had been through shone in their depths.

"No, Scooter!"

From the corner of Leo's eye, he saw Kristin get up and guide the dog over to the table before she sat back down and held him.

Drew's voice seemed to register with Kayla, and she found her purpose, the reason she'd come. "Look at how big you are."

Kayla's voice drifted off, choked with emotion. She stretched her hands out, a slight tremor showing through her fingers as she waited.

He swallowed, willing her children to accept her.

Ella had entered the room and gripped Annie's hand, her eyes wide. Drew went toward Kayla.

Leo didn't know what he had expected when they reunited, but this was pure joy. "Mama," Drew kept saying, patting Kayla on the arm.

Leo had seen how the adults took care to point out photos of Kayla and told Ella and Drew that was their mama. Now he understood.

Annie's eyes shimmered with tears, and she gently loosened Ella's hand, then gave her a nudge toward her mother and brother. The little girl stood there, and Leo held his breath. After what seemed like minutes but must have been seconds, she shuffled her way to her mother.

Ella leaned her little face close to Kayla's cheek and whispered "Mamma" over and over. Leo exhaled, only then becoming aware that he'd been holding his breath. Seeing them together warmed his heart in a way that almost burned with its strength.

Leo dragged his gaze from the little family. The others in the room had receded in his intense concentration of the moment. The sunlight had finally showed its face and beamed brightly through the window. The sun gave Kristin a kind of halo, made her look like an angel.

Annie remained rooted to the spot, and Leo's gut twisted as her gaze remained transfixed on the little reunited family. In what was probably only seconds, Annie pulled her attention from them, then walked away. Her pace picked up speed, and when she reached the opening that led back into the dining room, she bolted. Kristin sent a questioning look toward Leo and took a step toward following Annie. He gave the slightest nod, and she hurried in the direction Annie had gone.

# Chapter 11

Kristin's heartbeat picked up as she entered the dining area. Annie was nowhere to be seen. The hallways led to more rooms, and she didn't know where to start looking. She had no idea what she'd say to Annie when she located her. They didn't really know each other. Women experiencing heartache surrounding motherhood, that, she was familiar with. She had to try to help. A few steps into the hallway and she heard muffled sobs coming from behind one door.

She tapped two times. "Come in." Annie's voice was hushed yet sounded strong, which gave her hope.

The room was like an office with a desk and chair and short sofa, where Annie crashed on her back, cradling a pillow to her chest. She lifted her head at hearing the door click shut.

Kristin knelt on a rug beside the distraught woman, lightly

resting her hand on her back. *Help me, Lord.*

Annie shuddered on a sob. Her clogged throat strangled her words. "What are we going to do?"

"I have no answers. I wish I did. You have my full support, is all I'm here to say. I can't imagine what you're going through. But my life situation with having children has been more wrought than most. I don't know your exact pain but have been in places I thought would break me." She wasn't sure where these words were coming from, could only hope they might help in some way. "I've had to think about what it means to be a mother, more than most people."

Annie had stopped crying and gulped, then studied her with red-rimmed eyes. She got up and grabbed tissues from a box on the desk, then returned to the sofa and blew her nose.

"How did you sort it all? Figure out what was right? I don't want to be the bad guy here. My heart is broken in two."

"I do know every child is a gift from God, placed in our care. People say He loans them to us."

She nodded and blew her nose. "I knew this could happen. Kayla is recovered, a joyful thing, really. But what's most important, what matters, her health is what's best for Ella and Drew."

"Yes, you've already come a long way with accepting that. Whatever happens, you'll always be a mother of the heart for them. Blood connections have nothing to do with it. Besides, you're marrying Caleb and will always be their special aunt."

"Caleb will need me to be strong for him. We knew this was

always a possibility. We wanted Kayla to be well. I'm just not sure I really thought it through, how my heart would hurt. It's almost unbearable." Her tears flowed, and she wiped at her eyes with a tissue. "How will I tell Chloe?"

Her heart hurt thinking about that conversation. "You'll find a way. Kids are resilient. You'll get through." Kristin heard dishes landing on a table in the dining room, a welcome sound, signaling normal activity. Even people in emotional upheaval needed to eat, a reminder that they were all human. Although the idea of food didn't appeal.

"I've been where you are, with excruciating decisions to make. But there's time. Life will go on. You'll have conversations and consider options. There may be disagreements, maybe counseling? The point is, the power of prayer shows up in these times and you'll survive."

"How can we let them go? This is a big responsibility for her. Just like that, she has full custody. I asked around and heard that's how it is. But I can't believe it." Her tears began to flow again.

Kristin discreetly placed her hand on her stomach with its precious cargo. "You'll thrive again, as hard as that is to believe at this point. You all are strong, more than you know. These circumstances are what build character and a meaningful life. You're right in the thick of what family is all about."

Would she ever have a chance to be in a family again?

A light tap on the door interrupted her. She got up as the door cracked open and Caleb popped his head in, his eyes searching for Annie, until they locked on to one another. "We have so much to talk about. But first, let's have a good breakfast. Sierra is going to cook for us all."

The look they exchanged made Kristin feel like she was intruding on an intimate moment. He leaned down and spoke softly to her. As hard as what they were going through was, she envied that they had one another, that they would face this together.

What would it be like to have someone in her corner?

Annie stood up. She'd stopped crying and her eyes were red-rimmed but not too noticeable. She came over to Caleb and reached for his hand before they walked out together. Kristin trailed along, giving them their space.

It had been quite a day. Leo came up to her, so she asked him a neutral question, the tension in her chest getting lighter. "I'll need to know where your restroom is."

"When they renovated the main house in the spring, they installed another wing." He ushered her into the part of the house where he was staying.

She went right inside. When she had finished, she buttoned her pants and the button of her jeans popped off. What next? A safety pin might tide her over until she got home, and she wouldn't bother anyone. The fancy vanity on a pedestal with a marble countertop didn't have drawers. The medicine cabinet held her only hope. It felt like snooping, except there wasn't anything except bare necessities, like nail clippers. That's when she saw them, the opioids in Leo's medicine cabinet. No safety pins either. They had different, fancy names, but the prescription had been made out to Leo in the beginning of July. If he was addicted, surely these would be gone by now.

What did she really know about him? How did he live his life now? Because their childhood had been a long time ago. She had no clue. The anguish of Craig's addiction, including the sneaking around he did to hide it, gripped her heart. Could Leo be going through something similar? She couldn't see how that could be. She and Craig had been having major problems and were not compatible before the drugs. He'd taken her away from Fair Creek, from family.

Was she being naïve to think that she could still have a happy relationship, maybe even marriage?

If she had thought there was a chance of that, she might have made a different choice with implanting her embryos. *Trust me.* Things were obviously meant to be how they were turning out. She couldn't have moved on and be happy if she had made any other choice except giving them a chance at life to become her family.

She had to face how drawn she was to Leo. He seemed fond of her. Did his feelings go deeper?

Everything was in God's hands, and all she could do was wait. Unfortunately, she'd never been a patient person.

# Chapter 12

Leo moved his paint roller up and down the community room wall at Miracle Mommies. The rhythm of the work soothed him. After two days of stewing over Kristin's last conversation with him, he'd come to no conclusions. So, he'd used the key she'd given him the night she hired him and started the work.

He'd set up his phone to play music from his high school days to keep him company. This assignment was supposed to be low-key, and that's what it would be. But the situation with his employer rivaled that in his heaviest season for commissioned art.

Not that he thought of Kristin as his employer exactly. She was a family friend, a single mom having triplets. Happened every day.

A sound came from somewhere in the front of the house. Leo continued laying the malted milk ball shade onto the wall. Likely, Kristin had shown up. His heart rate picked up just thinking of her.

How could she have that effect on him, under the circumstances, including that he wasn't interested in a relationship and wasn't staying home long? But he wasn't going to question it. He finished on a corner, a good place to stop. Maybe he should go investigate. He put his roller down in the tray.

Kristin strolled into the room in a navy T-shirt with "cowgirl" written on the front in white scripted letters. "Good morning. Came by to drop off a throw my friend crocheted. I crochet too." She went to the hallway closet and deposited a baby-blue blanket made of yarn on the shelf.

She looked at it sitting there. "Oh, wait, you'll just have to move it when you paint in there. Duh."

He picked up the roller, needing something to do with his hands so he didn't hug her. "Thought that must be you. I was about to go see." He'd wanted to see her, and now it felt…awkward.

"I'm getting around a little more slowly, just going with the flow, you could say."

Even if he was uncertain how he felt about her being a mother, he wanted her to be okay. What was the proper thing to do in this circumstance? "I've been thinking that you shouldn't be around paint fumes."

*Right, fall into your professional painter mode.*

Nothing to do but go on. "I've cracked the windows and will

really air the room out well. You can relax and crochet, make your plans or whatever."

"Thank you for getting started, and for considering my needs. Why don't I set up in the screened-in back porch attached to the kitchen? There's a sofa, the only furniture."

"You'll be spared the paint fumes. You might freeze to death."

Her lips turned up, and the strained look on her face disappeared. "So, there's that, huh? Life's a tradeoff, they say. Okay, I've brought a nice, industrial heater. The walls in there aren't well-insulated."

She whipped out her phone. "I checked the weather app, and we're in for a cold snap through Christmas day. I've brought a parka to wear, if I need it."

"Doesn't sound real cozy."

"You're wanting to relax here. Well, so am I." She reached in a canvas bag and pulled out yarn in some kind of shape he couldn't identify. "Let me introduce you to my crocheted milk cow. It's even spotted like a Guernsey."

This was a different mood than he'd seen her in. "Well, what do ya know? If your fingers don't get too numb, you'll have a homemade baby toy in the end."

She returned the strange thing to her bag and leaned so close he caught a whiff of her soapy scent. "I've never sat that still in my life, honestly. It about killed me to do the cow's face."

"Imagine that, and it just looks like some kind of yarn art to me."

A slight frown and combination pout played around her lips.

"How could you not have recognized it?" She was so adorable when she showed her true self, always had been.

"Look, I feel for you, having to slow down. It's about like waiting for glaciers to melt for me to be back in Fair Creek. Partly, my counselor told me I needed to relax more, but there's a limit, you know?"

"What? You're here under doctor's orders?" She paused, and when he didn't fill in the gap, she went on. "We'll just have to keep one another entertained, then. I'll go nuts if I hang around over there at my place. Please don't make me."

As the words left her mouth, her eyes lit up. He'd forgotten how fun their teasing had been.

"Of course, I won't. Solidarity and all that."

Time to make amends, while they were enjoying themselves.

"I've been wanting to tell you that I might not have handled things well, at first, with your pregnancy news." He didn't think he'd done all that badly, although there had been room for improvement. "But how are you doing? You're carrying new life. Three of them. Who wouldn't be excited at that?"

Some of the tension that had crackled in the air between them on the subject had dissipated. "My doctor told me to go easy. It's still very early but, with my medical history, I'm in a high-risk pregnancy, and I'm going to be extra careful. I'm strictly following orders."

She waved her hand, signaling to switch topics. Her nails were more ragged than before, and it jogged his memory. As a girl, she'd bitten her nails when she was nervous.

"How's the painting going?"

"Taking me longer than expected. Even basically painting empty rooms has its tricks. You can see where I taped around the trim to protect the wood. But it's coming along. I've done the preliminary preparation for the murals."

She noticed some colors and sketches on the walls. She picked up a spare brush from the pack he'd tossed to the side. His chest tightened. "Don't even think about it." It wasn't really any of his business. Was it? No matter who it was in this situation, he would be removing the brush from their hand in her condition. But he already cared about her—and them—more than he wanted to.

"As much as I'd enjoy painting side by side with you, that's not really an option." When he grabbed onto the paintbrush handle, his fingers grazed her knuckles. Soft, smooth skin connected with his, and he lingered a moment.

She released the handle. "You're right. This is all new for me, and I'm probably a little in shock, especially given the circumstances. You know me. There's a lot to do here, and I want to be in every part of it."

He went and stood at the other end of the big double windows. A hill with snow on it drew his attention when he noticed they had shared fences. Her property bordered Galloway Farm in the distance. He hadn't remembered them being quite that close. Something in him wanted to be connected with her, in whatever ways possible.

"How about this? I'll set you up in a room that's painted and aired out. After I finish this one, I'm going to get some paint I've read about that's nearly odorless. You can choose whatever room you want, to be like your office. I'll keep you informed of what's going on. If you need anything, I'll be right here."

She smiled and her deep-blue eyes dazzled him. "You don't need to take care of me. I hired you for painting."

"Maybe I just expanded my job description, if you'll let me."

"You've proposed an amazing plan, honestly. There's a lot I can do with my computer and phone, making calls and ordering what I'll need." She shrugged. "I just like being here."

"So, you're on board?"

"You sure this isn't going to add to your pressures or anything? You came here for downtime, and now you've thrown yourself into this project, my dream really."

Her eyes sparkled, and he wanted to understand, and maybe even feel what she felt. But he just didn't.

"This is so different from my high-stress commissioned work that I'll be fine."

She touched his sleeve, and he could feel her warmth before she pulled away. "Good. I can't wait to see the changes painting the walls will make in here."

"I know. Even after all of these years of working with my art, I'm still amazed at how color brings out such emotion and shapes moods."

Kristin reached out her hand, flecked off lint or something. "I'll be mixing business with pleasure. It's so great to renew our friendship. When things have gone wrong in a person's life, the way they have in mine, there's extra comfort in going back to the beginning."

"That all sounds fine with me. I'm enjoying getting to know each other as adults. Yet there's so much of the girl I used to know—your strong spirit and determination. You haven't chosen an easy path. But there's no doubt in my mind you'll be a terrific mother."

He sure hoped business would be enough. Against his better judgment, he longed for more.

The Indiana air must be getting to him. Smog might be good for squelching unrealistic expectations.

She put her hand on his arm again and looked into his eyes. The depth of her feelings he saw there drew him in until he finally pulled his hand away and dropped his gaze. He wanted to get to know her better, so much so that it scared him.

He'd never had a romantic relationship work out. The few he had all started with promise, some more than others. But the endings had devastated him. He didn't think he could survive that again, especially not with her. Being on his own was better. Safer.

He plastered on a smile and stood. "This room isn't going to paint itself. Better get back to your room, away from the fumes."

The sooner he finished the painting, the quicker he would be away from the temptation of being around her.

For some reason, that thought didn't bring him any satisfaction.

# Chapter 13

Kristin opened her eyes and tried to orient herself. The rock-hard sofa beneath her could mean only one thing. She'd fallen asleep in the sunroom at Miracle Mommies. She sat up, made sure the crochet project in her lap was unharmed as she put it aside, and stretched out her arms. Her smart phone said she'd slept for around three hours.

To reach the bathroom, she passed the room Leo stood painting in. Either he didn't notice because he was concentrating on his work, or because he was daydreaming, but she didn't disturb him. When she was done in the bathroom, she searched the toiletries for unexpected visitors she'd stashed in a cabinet and found a toothbrush to use.

It wasn't because of Leo. She just liked to have fresh breath after she awakened.

*Yeah, right.*

She popped in to where Leo painted. He must have forgotten to remove his cowboy hat, but she appreciated that he hadn't. He seemed to put an unusual amount of focus into the work. She took the chance to peek at his profile, especially his strong jaw line with a hint of stubble she hadn't noticed before.

"Can I fix you some lunch?"

She must have startled him because he didn't have a chance to school his expression. His dark-brown eyes lit up upon seeing it was her.

"Sleeping Beauty cooks?"

His voice seemed a little bit deeper than before, maybe from lack of use. The divine resonance of it sent a thrill through her.

*Grow up.*

So, he had checked on her. Hopefully, she hadn't drooled—or snored. Why did she care? She wasn't going to analyze why; she just did.

"If heating up leftover crockpot chili qualifies? Then yes."

They decided he'd paint while she got things ready. She'd made an easy crockpot chili recipe yesterday, the only thing she'd accomplished all day. For some reason, she'd brought the leftovers and put them in the refrigerator after she and Aunt Jackie had their fill. There was even a handful of snickerdoodles in a bag from the Sweet Shop Bakery.

*Admit it. You hoped he'd show up today.*

Adding lettuce to two bowls and sprigs of vegetables, she called to him in the adjoining room. "Ready in a minute."

After he'd put his painting away, she assumed, she heard the bathroom water running and he came into the kitchen.

"You're spoiling me. I packed a P.B. and J. in a lunchbox in the truck."

There was that special twinkle in his eyes again. Was he flirting with her? Maybe he didn't know what he was doing and these feelings were only on her end. She made a thing of concentrating on the pathetic little pile of vegetables she was calling a salad.

He wouldn't let her help clear off the printer table and bring it to the sofa. She'd planned on standing at the bar, but he wanted to sit.

"Sorry. I'll bring some chairs and barstools. Starting from scratch, and it's hard to believe all we need." Thank goodness she'd remembered to bring good utensils from the basket set that was designed to take on picnics, even down to a tablecloth that was included.

She started to cover the little table, and he grabbed one end and helped spread it out. They each carried some food over and managed to get it all to fit on the table.

"Guess we'll have to eat on the sofa and hold our plates in our laps," he said, not looking unhappy at all.

An excuse to sit next to each other appealed to her. He seemed to imply he felt the same.

When they'd filled their plates, she sat cowdn in one corner, and Leo filled his corner and more. She'd forgotten how large a man he was. One muscled thigh nearly touched hers. Her stomach fluttered at his closeness. His clean, woodsy scent wafted into her nose.

"I'd forgotten this is a loveseat, not a full-sized sofa."

Well, that hadn't been a great thing to say.

His eyes seemed to have an extra sparkle, and the distance between them was nonexistent so she could see the golden flecks in them. "This is perfect. May I offer a blessing?"

His brief prayer covered the food, her pregnancy, and their friendship, in few words. She added an "amen" after his. The tension in her shoulders eased.

He waved his fork, pointing around the room, before spiking some lettuce. "Why is this so important to you? You've gotten what you wanted. There's a lot ahead of you. No one would blame you if you stepped back from Miracle Mommies."

She swallowed water to tamp down her annoyance. "You don't understand. This is more than a 4H project for the judges or to keep myself busy, Leo. I wasn't doing it to remove the ache of my not having a baby. Once I was in that place, of the real possibility I couldn't have kids, I knew I'd help others, even if things changed for me. My faith kept me going. Others don't have that. Community is important for all of us, and I wanted to provide that, and I still do."

She took a bite of chili, grateful for the ease in which they talked with one another.

"You have a calling. I did, too, though I didn't get much support for it."

"I want to support you. Being a creative isn't always a stable environment though. With kids, I think about the whole picket fence thing, which I don't have. At my level, it's more like being an entrepreneur, and I have the commissions to manage and the actual artwork, so I've kept my head down and pushed hard for years. Maybe it's my dad in my head, telling me what a poor career choice I was making. Mom wasn't as vocal about it, but I was treated like the one who wouldn't amount to anything. What did I expect when my talents were so outside their experience? Now that I've succeeded beyond my wildest expectations, maybe it's time to get rid of those old tapes in my head."

He directed his gaze toward the bakery bag and leaned over. "Cookie time." Not waiting for permission, he pulled out two cookies, gave one to her, then took a bite from his.

They munched in silence, faces so close she wondered what it would be like if their lips met.

With one finger, he reached out to the edge of her mouth. "There's a big crumb right here." He picked up the stray piece of cookie and held it to her lips and she gobbled it up.

Kristin moved back into her corner of the sofa and hoped her cheeks weren't flushed. Her heartbeat picked up in a way it hadn't around a man in a long time, maybe ever.

Leo just went right on. "With my work, the scenes I get to paint and the places I've been, I'm always taken aback when clients say they aren't believers. I want to say, '*Really*?' All that beauty." He held the bag out. "Here, you want another one?"

"My resistance is low." And that applied to cookies and cowboys. Two squirrels chased each other around the tree branches outside the window. She took a cookie.

"It's too bad your parents didn't appreciate your accomplishments, your talent. That can make it hard. Getting a divorce isn't something I ever wanted. It's taken me years to accept that it wasn't just the result of my failures. For a long time, I felt that someone else who was more devoted, had stronger faith, or fill-in-the-blank, could have made it work."

He broke the last cookie in two and they finished it off together. "I'm sorry. None of that's true, but I can see how you'd think that. As an overachiever, which I thought you were called in your yearbook, that had to be especially rough."

Kristin stood and started gathering plates. These topics had left her unsettled. Part of her still felt she was bad at relationships. She picked the things up and, although Leo tried to help, she shooed him into the other room to resume painting. With a leftover paper plate, she fanned her face and enjoyed the distraction of watching a tractor from Galloway Farm in their back field.

Her plan to have Leo paint this place might be an exercise in resisting the cowboy's good looks and charm.

# Chapter 14

While Leo did his afternoon painting work, he could hear Kristin's voice as a murmur in the back. Good thing they were separated in the house or he might end up joining her on the loveseat again. His powers of control might not be as strong this time around. Eating cookies had reminded him of all their after-school snacks, except she was no longer a schoolgirl. Not even close.

He checked his watch. Time for his midafternoon break. After taking care of his workspace, he went looking for Kristin in the back.

From the entrance to the sunroom, the way she was seated on the sofa while she spoke on the phone took his breath. Sunlight poured in from all directions, and she was too busy jotting down the occasional note and talking to notice him staring. Her turned-up nose and pale skin had made her a cute child and now contributed to the beautiful woman before him.

She was talking about the flooring that would be installed after he finished the walls. He was making good progress and was going to be sorry to be gone from her, for some reason.

What was wrong with him? He'd better snap out of it. She was expecting babies, and he'd be long gone by then, back to his work.

She hung up and he moved right into the room as though he hadn't been standing there.

"Flooring's all on schedule. How's it going with the painting?"

"I'm ahead of where I expected to be at this point, actually."

A look came into her eyes, more like a shadow. He wondered if she wanted him to stay too. Must be his imagination. "That's great. I've been hitting it pretty hard. I'm about to take a crochet break. Care to join me? I can chat as I go."

She scooted over on the loveseat. Oh, how he wanted to sit beside her. Instead, he took a seat on the floor nearby.

"You're good at multi-tasking, which will come in handy I would think." He didn't want to really talk about the babies but alluding to them kept him grounded. Dating wasn't a possibility for them, even if he had wanted to, which he didn't.

She arranged her yarn and hook to start. "Oh, now I just read that studies show it's better to focus on one thing at a time."

"That figures. When will they study the advantages of not doing studies, is what I want to know?"

She laughed, a tinkling sound he couldn't get enough of when she was a kid. Back then she had always laughed long and hard, especially for such a little girl.

While she crocheted a row of stitches, silence hung between them. She came to the end and picked up her pattern, holding it between her fingers. "How come a great guy like you isn't taken?"

"I'm not sure how to answer that. I've been taken before, depending on what you mean. Unfortunately, my bank account attracts the wrong kind of female attention sometimes."

The open, honest look in her eyes stopped him cold, waiting for her response. "Fair enough. What about love?"

For a minute there, he'd wanted her to choose him. He must be losing it.

She repositioned herself on the sofa, and a ball of yarn rolled off onto the floor. He reached down to get it at the exact same time she did. Inches from one another, their eyes locked.

He picked up the yarn. Maybe it was the sun making anything seem possible and everything magical. But the rough texture on his fingers stirred his senses. "I'm not sure I'm as great a guy as you deserve. Do you have any idea how long I've waited for a kiss?"

The nod was so slight he wasn't sure if it happened at all. Then his lips were on hers and he had his answer. He leaned into the softness of her lips, which fit his perfectly. He let go of the yarn and rested his arm lightly on her shoulder. She tasted of sweetness, the sugar and cinnamon of the cookies. When she came closer and pressed her mouth to his, the sensation was his best kiss in a long while, probably ever.

When Kristin pulled away, her voice sounded throatier. "We better, uh, see how the painting's going?"

Who cared? She'd just melted his socks off. "Slow, actually. I'm having focus issues."

Kristin's face turned pink. She opened her mouth and no words came out.

"You too, huh? Maybe you better stay and crochet."

He resumed his work, and a couple of hours later, he noticed Kristin standing in the doorway. Her eyes matched the deep blue of the sky outside the window and had an extra sparkle somehow. Had he put it there?

"Sorry about the interruption." Now her cheeks were pink. "I mean, for standing here while I'm supposed to be letting you work. You know, the thing about this place is, it's something I'm supposed to be involved in."

"I've sometimes heard people who never had kids talk about what they will do instead. Miracle Mommies would have been that for me, except now I'll have kids, too." Her smile looked happy and reached up to her eyes. "I feel guilty sometimes that Craig will miss out. When things were good, he wanted kids as much as I did. Only thing is, he wasn't a very supportive partner, or maybe men can't really understand going through the infertility treatments. Either way, now because of this place, women will have extra help."

"I haven't been that invested in anything I've ever done, other than maybe my art. I do think of it as a God-given talent I'm supposed to use. The Bible story about the talents stayed with me since I was young."

"I think we heard that one together! Remember the little kids' Sunday school teacher was sick and we combined with the big kids?"

"I really don't. I think I dreaded those situations. Sorry."

"Well, the younger set is always excited to be moved up with the older ones. Honestly, here with you, I'm feeling a little of that."

His heart skipped a beat, and he knew he was done. "Guess I'm going to quit for the day. So then does that mean you'll agree to go to my brothers' weddings with me? You'll get them off my back about bringing someone. Not sure what's in it for you."

She shrugged. "spending the evening with you."

"Thanks."

"See you tomorrow for the ultrasound appointment."

Before he could express doubts, she walked out. After a few seconds, he thought he heard a little squeal come from the sunroom.

This ultrasound had him concerned. He could surely do this one thing for Heath's little sister without getting deeply entangled. All his life, he'd been the one who came through when someone needed him.

Kristin brought out the trait in him even more than most people did. He'd gotten better about boundaries, as the relationship experts called it.

Something told him he'd need that ability more than ever in his near future.

# Chapter 15

In the two days since Leo had offered to go with Kristin to the ultrasound appointment, he had been in avoidance mode. He'd found excuses not to paint at Miracle Mommies or be out where he might run into her. But this morning, the day of the appointment, he got up extra early to finish the farm chores so he could be sure to pick up Kristin in time. The knot in his stomach since the moment he'd awakened stayed put. What had possessed him to go to her appointment?

*Lord, help all to go well. Your will be done.*

If he'd thought of another prayer, he would've prayed it.

In the mudroom, he pulled on his heavy coat and boots, then added a face covering under his cowboy hat for good measure. When he pushed the exterior door open, the cold still hit his nostrils when he stepped out onto the ground at the back door.

The sudden burst of chilly air jogged his memory and he whirled around, heading back inside for a carrot and an apple he'd stored in the fridge to give Louise, the horse who had become his favorite, and her foal. Then he retraced his steps and made his way to the horse barn.

A peace came over him as he walked, and his stomach settled. What was this about? He hadn't been crazy about being assigned farm duties, not after all this time. What was the point? He wasn't sure how long he'd be here, but he definitely wouldn't see springtime.

He went into the horse stall and patted Louise's nose. Then he put the apple in the palm of his hand as he'd been told as a small child. Guess being around horses and everything on the farm was like riding a bike. You really didn't forget.

By the time he had visited with both of them for a couple of minutes and finished all of his chores, he had warmed up a bit from the outside. Their large bodies were no doubt throwing off some heat.

The alarm on his smart watch rang. Time to go so he could get cleaned up before he left. Lingering, he inhaled the straw and animal scents. The barn felt homey, and he patted each animal a couple more times. This surprised him, the desire to be in here at all, let alone feeling a pull to stay a while longer.

He prayed for understanding of his change of heart. It seemed to be happening in several ways, the most obvious being that he'd agreed to go to this doctor's appointment at all. He'd never had a problem saying no to anyone. So, what was it about Kristin that brought out all the "yes" in him he'd never noticed?

He had a therapy session by phone every couple of weeks because his therapist had insisted. But he didn't find the need to reach out to go over things like he had before. Apparently, this short shift in his lifestyle had done him good. He felt closer to God here, too, not that he hadn't when he painted, but the pressures surrounding his work always seemed to press in on him.

His watch alarm vibrated on his wrist, his reminder to get a move on. "See you, gals." He walked away from the horses.

He showered off and changed into his clothes. The shirt he'd laid out was one Kristin had complimented him on. He wouldn't think why he remembered or why that mattered.

On the way to his car, he whistled a tune from his boyhood about a dog named BINGO for some reason he didn't understand.

The several minutes it took to get to Kristin's went too quickly, and before he knew it, she was hopping in his truck. The conversation was limited. Once Kristin had checked in at the doctor's office, they sat side by side, scrolling on their phones. If something came up on their screens, they shared it with one another. It almost could have been like a casual date, except the reason they were there was all too real. Kristin glanced around the room. The art on the walls were all cheap prints like Van Gogh's Irises. He wondered if she was feeling this closeness too.

"Kristin Barclay?" The nurse's call-out pulled his brain back to the present.

Kristin stood and was almost to the inner door when she

looked back at him and motioned with her hand for him to come, too.

He mouthed the words, "You sure you want me there?"

Her nod was such a small movement anyone else might have missed it. Leo stood. He tried to form the words of a prayer but nothing came. But "help" kept running through his mind like a mantra.

Why had he come? A confirmed bachelor had no place here where girlfriends belonged. Or a husband. Annie had been through childbirth, the perfect candidate.

*Stop thinking about yourself. Imagine how she's feeling.* But he had no idea what might be going through her mind. All he knew is that he shouldn't be here. Not for a momentous occasion, no matter how this went down. She had tried to prepare him, that infertility treatment involved viewing and checking the embryos much earlier than most pregnant women did. The gold standard was getting past the first trimester, and some people waited to tell others outside their immediate circle until that all-important date had passed.

Leo watched her go in and stood outside of the exam room door while she changed. When she was ready, she tapped on the door as they had agreed. He entered with reluctance, and by the time he was in the room, she was on the exam table covered in a sheet.

The big smile she gave him made it worth it for him to be here—almost, anyway. Maybe he was as nervous as she was.

"Well, I'm glad somebody is prepared. Not sure how you

talked me into this. Oh, I volunteered."

"Maybe I softened you by looking at the new kitties with you, or was it the snickerdoodles. Come over here, please. You look a little green." He followed her instructions and stood by her side. "Take my hand."

Like she was precious property, he gently clasped her hand. It had never felt so delicate, so vulnerable. "You're cold or is that shivering caused by something else?"

"You ask too many questions."

A tap on the door and the technician, nurse, or whatever, entered. He moved to a corner of the room. She acknowledged him standing there, said congratulations like he was the dad.

"I'm Leo Galloway, just her big brother's best friend." Well, where had that come from? Talk about distancing himself from the situation.

He took off his Stetson, patted his hair down, and replaced it. He might have shoved the hat down a little more, hiding his face. He should have thought it through better before agreeing to go to this appointment.

But the woman seemed unaware of his discomfort and moved right along to putting on gloves, calibrating the machine, and preparing a wand thing. He relocated to a seat at the side of the room where he wouldn't see anything private and focused on the screen.

When the images came on the machine, he couldn't look away. These were tiny humans in fluid. The medical specialist guided the instrument, and when she saw the first image resembling babies, like he'd seen in ultrasound photos women carried proudly, she measured it and drew a circle around it.

"Baby number one." She directed the pointer to a specific area. "See that small flash that keeps coming nice and steady? That's the heartbeat."

The woman spoke in calm tones, exuding competence that he found comforting. When he looked over at Kristin, she gave him a smile through quivering lips.

Leo swallowed the lump in his throat. He needed to do something. But what? He went over and held her hand, which was cold and trembling. He leaned down and murmured in her ear, "You're going to make a wonderful mother." He knew without a shadow of a doubt that she would. If he ever had kids, she would be his choice to be their mom.

Except he wasn't going to have any. An ache went through him. It was a sensation he'd never had before when he thought about not having children.

Could God have other plans for him? He wasn't sure.

Kristi's hand seemed to be absorbing heat from his, and he gave her a little squeeze as the medical facts unfolded.

The technician's professional tone continued, like she was unaware of all that was going on in the room, as she should be. "Here's baby number two."

Leo swallowed. He looked around the room like it was sacred space. Maybe it was. These didn't have to be his babies for the importance of the moment to take hold.

After going through the same motions another time, the

woman took a few more measurements, which involved checking the size of the embryos' heads and other details and completed the exam. She left.

The silent room put them in a holding pattern. "Have you already thought of names?"

Kristin smiled. "As a matter of fact, I've had a mental list going since I made this decision. Guess I'll need more than one."

The doctor came in. "Congratulations, Ms. Barclay. I'm aware of what you've been through to achieve pregnancy. However, I would be remiss if I didn't tell you there are additional risks to multiples, and some of my patients choose to undergo fetal reduction."

She frowned and shook her head. "Oh, I couldn't. No."

"If you're sure, then I'm encouraged to report that your good health and what we've seen so far puts you in an optimum condition to deliver three healthy babies."

He described when she would be out of his care and be referred back to her regular obstetrician. More details went over his head. Three little children would be coming into the world. That was enough to grasp.

The doctor shook Leo's hand on his way out. "Going to need three sets of tiny cowboy boots."

The other medical person cleaned up or whatever they did, then left.

"Will you be all right if I leave while you change?"

Kristin's coloring nearly matched the sheet. She nodded.

Once in the hallway outside, the enormity of the situation hit

Leo like a ton of paint cans. He was grateful he would be leaving to let her change. Beads of perspiration accumulated under his cowboy hat in a way he couldn't remember lately, if ever.

He massaged his forehead, wondering if the tension was the start of a headache. Kristin's babies weren't his responsibility. So where was this guilt coming from, like he was shirking his duties? They were both single, and he cared deeply for her. How far did that extend?

The door of the exam room opened, and Kristin came out fully dressed.

Kristi squeezed his hand. "Three miracles." She inhaled.

Words came from his mouth, surprising him. "God doesn't give us more than we can handle." He'd never been sure about that, not really, and wasn't convinced it applied here.

Once again, he wondered at the wisdom of coming to this appointment. It felt like the first step to involvement with the babies.

He would have to draw a line, but how? He couldn't say what he would be willing to do or not do.

# Chapter 16

In the hospital parking lot, Kristin put her foot on the running board of Leo's truck and wondered how many diapers three babies wore in a month. A lot! Leo stood with the door open, and she hoisted herself in, taking comfort from the heated seat.

Braces. Both she and Heath had terrible overbites corrected. What would these kids' orthodontist's bills be?

A shadow of concern crossed Leo's face and a crease in his forehead became more pronounced. "There's a lot to think about, isn't there?"

It had always seemed they could read one another's minds as kids. He knew her too well. "I'm a planner, but this is outside of the realm of anything I've ever dealt with."

"It's easy for me to say, but most of us are capable of much more than we realize."

Leo walked around to the driver's side and in seconds appeared on the seat across from her. His smile didn't reach up to his eyes.

"Being pushed to my limit isn't something I look forward to."

He rubbed his chin and shook his head with nothing more to say. How was she hurting Leo by drawing him into this? The man was supposed to be relaxing.

He started the truck. "If anyone is able to do something like this, it's you. It's natural to feel overwhelmed when everything's new, a totally unknown experience."

She held her head in her hands, giving up the appearance of having it all together. "What am I going to do?"

Her voice sounded a bit strangled in her ears. A tension came up between them, silence where she wanted words.

Finally, he spoke. "I thought you'd maybe made arrangements of some kind, since you heard the preliminary findings a week ago."

She raised her head. "How could I possibly prepare for this? I never dreamed there would be one baby, let alone three."

He started the truck like he was ready to move on. "Well, didn't they tell you triplets were a possibility?"

"Definitely. It's just, you have no idea how many discussions I've had with doctors over the years, how many times there were no babies. The methods and procedures we did were endless, the timing of it bad to awful. Once, we missed the family Easter gathering for a doctor procedure. Another time it was the Barclay Christmas gift exchange, all because we were tied to charts, cycles, and test results. It all starts to sound like mumbo jumbo when they say it could be a baby or there could be multiples, like some statement written by lawyers, not real. It never had happened before to my ex and me. Not once in four years."

"I'm sorry. I thought you wanted to be pregnant."

"Now? Being a single mom terrifies me. I wanted to do the right thing in God's sight. Never dreamed he had single motherhood in mind."

Leo kept his eyes on the road, and she was glad not to feel the need to talk as they headed back to Fair Creek in silence.

*Lord.*

The next words wouldn't come. God knew her needs, and she had to trust. Gazing out of the truck window at the vastness of open fields dusted with snow spoke to her. Her shoulders relaxed and she took deep breaths. They were almost to town when her eyes fluttered open.

"Hopefully, a little rest did you good." Leo had concern in his eyes, and that was what she needed, apparently.

A smile crept onto her lips, and she laid her hand on his arm, so nice and solid. "Your being here for me is the best medicine."

She knew she had people who cared, but something about the depth of him, just his presence back in her life, made all the difference.

"Where are we headed? Need dropped off back at your place? Breakfast?"

"Would you mind coming to Delaney's with me? If we got done at the doctor's early enough, I said I'd go over there.

Some friends are pitching in to help me with items for Miracle Mommies."

There was no reason for Leo to come, except she had a physical need for him to be with her.

"If you're up to it, sounds good to me."

She let out her breath. Things were going to be fine. She didn't know how, but she had to believe.

Coming into town, the wreaths on the decorative light poles lining both sides of the street and the big, community Christmas tree in a paved lot in the middle of town put her in the holiday spirit. Winter greenery filled the flowerpots on every corner.

"We're so lucky to be in this wonderful place, or do you not feel that way?"

He looked over at her, his brown eyes intense. "I'm beginning to. At least through your eyes I do, for now."

A few minutes later, he parked the truck at the curb on Main Street. The diner's door and big windows on both sides had a primitive, painted nativity scene across the expanse. The primary colors, with the bright yellow star and navy night sky warmed her heart. But the baby in the manger put a lump in her throat, and she fought back tears.

Leo looked across the windows and his eyes sparkled as he breathed his response in her ear. "Sometimes, the simple really is beautiful, isn't it?"

By the time Leo escorted her in and Kristin stepped into Delanie's Diner, she was struck once again by how much had stayed the same, as she was six months before.

The scent of bacon and the sounds of voices shored her up. The pit in her stomach since the triplets were confirmed eased off. Nearly every seat was filled, and familiar faces surrounded her in a warm splash of recognition.

Sierra Delaney hurried over and gave her a quick hug. "Hey, still can't believe how good it is having you back in town." They had never been close, but Fair Creek was so small, their paths had crossed in school. Coming from the same place gave them something in common.

Annie walked up to them. Her blonde hair was always the color of wheat, and the sun streaming through the big picture window made her stand out. "Can I bring you something?"

The last time she'd seen Annie had been at the farm when Kayla returned. Maybe Annie's eyes looked a little dark underneath. She wondered how things were going. She initiated a hug with Annie, taking her in and hanging on just a little bit longer than necessary. "A tall glass of lemonade sounds wonderful."

She'd be limiting her caffeine for a while. Annie went for the refreshment, and Kristin took a real look around the room and found who she'd come for. A group of women had pushed two tables together and all sat doing needlework of some kind.

"Just the people I wanted to see." Smiling at their dear faces came as naturally as breathing. "With you all in my corner, there's nothing I can't do."

Leo carried a chair over for her from the far wall. She felt heat rising to her cheeks as he hovered nearby until she was seated comfortably.

"Who said chivalry's dead?" Bree Mason, a newish Fair Creek High graduate, had just returned to save the museum and didn't look up from crocheting a baby cap.

Relieved that Leo had gone over to speak with a table of men, Kristin settled into her favorite topic. "So, what's the scoop on how your assignment's going, ladies."

Annie brought her a glass of lemonade. "Here's a little something on the house." The plate of scrambled eggs and toast with apple butter—her favorite—on the side spoke to her stomach and it growled. Annie slipped away before she could thank her.

People called out, and she ate, suddenly starving.

"This is my second lap shawl."

"I'm making beaded bracelets that say 'grace' on them. I thought that was a nice, neutral message and applies to so much of what I would imagine infertility patients go through."

Sherry Fine owned the soap and candle shop and was putting the finishing flourish on a bow that decorated a ceramic, claw-footed tub filled with candle wax with a wick sticking up.

"I'm so glad you're letting all of us be a part of this."

"Oh, I'm the one who is grateful. Look at you all, working away. Actually, I tucked my crochet into my bag, and now all I'm doing is shoving food into my face. You know, this is like an old-fashioned quilting bee!"

Natalie Bogue, choir director and associate pastor at Fair Creek Community, spoke. "We said a prayer before we started, that our efforts will bless your ministry."

Kristin touched her hand over her heart. "You have no idea

how much that means to me."

There was a pause in the chatter, and she looked around.

A voice at the far end of the table sounded out. "Is there anything you'd like to share with us? We don't want to intrude." Shirley Leap scooted her chair back and stood up.

"Sure we do. We're dying to know. What did the doctor say?"

All eyes around the table rested on Kristin. The conversations and dishes clanking had disappeared, and it seemed as though the entire dining room had gone silent.

She stood and went over beside Shirley. "I'm going to be a mother." Only the women at the table could hear.

The sounds around the room seemed to start up again. Might as well get it over with. She told her friends, the women near her. "Future mother of three babies. I'm carrying triplets."

Shirley hollered it out like she was at a rodeo. "Hey, everybody, it's triplets!"

The entire community in the diner erupted into clapping, and the ladies left their chairs and rushed Kristin. They wrapped her in their arms and patted her back, one kissed her on the forehead. It was like one great big, warm hug. Once things had settled down, she thanked them again for their work and went over to find Leo.

"You need to hitch a ride?" he asked her since he'd seen her making her way over in the fairly small room.

"Whenever you're ready. I don't want to rush you." When she reached the table, he stood and patted her arm, like a friend. Nothing more. An ache made its way into her chest, but there was no reason for it. She was on her own, as she'd been the past several years, and everybody knew it.

She'd better get used to it.

Now that she'd had a taste of spending time with Leo, a wish had opened up that she'd long given up on. Wanting to be part of a couple.

"Kristin, come here a minute before we go. You remember Ted Mitchell?"

She knew the name but wasn't really sure. "I think so. How are you, Ted?

A man with a ball cap on his head that was emblazoned with some farm logo stood there, white hair peeking out underneath his hat. "I knew your granny. I remember you when you were just a little tyke." He held his hand down by his knee.

Leo came up and wrapped his arm lightly around Kristin's shoulders. His warmth comforted her after what seemed like a long day, even though it was only late afternoon.

"Ted's wife passed away a few years ago," Leo said. "He and some guys are fixtures here in the mornings, solving the world's problems over coffee. Recently, he began seeing my Aunt Elizabeth."

"I don't think I've met Elizabeth," Kristin said.

Ted chimed in. "You're in for a treat when you do. Too bad I can't say the same about Leo." He let out a hearty laugh. "You better watch the company you keep, young lady."

When Leo joined in the laughter, she did too. This was a side of him she hadn't seen.

"I knew I was taking a risk by bringing Kristin over here," he said. "You know all my secrets."

Ted slapped Leo on the back. "I'm not serious. Leo's really a pretty good guy. We like him."

They stood there a minute and then Ted spoke in a quieter tone.

"My wife would have loved that you're having triplets. She knitted a baby blanket for every child born in these parts since the 70s."

"She sounds special. I'm sorry for your loss."

"You know what, I think she had made extra blankets, always prepared for a new little one. I'll look, Kristin. Who knows where she might have stashed them? Sure do miss her. It'd certainly be nice to keep up that blanket tradition. Oh and another thing, my great granddaughter heard your presentation at the hospital support group. What do you call your place again?"

"Miracle Mommies House."

"Well, my friends and I are always looking for causes to support. Somebody proposed that we see what we can do for you."

"That would be terrific. I'm just getting started and am figuring out what we need. There are items that don't cost much and others that are quite high. I need to finalize the figures. Really appreciate your generosity."

Ted said, "I like helping people, keeping it local when we can."

Leo had been looking around and must be ready to leave.

"It was so nice meeting you," she said to the others.

Her feet were moving, and she put on her friendliest good-bye smile.

It had been nice to be part of a couple, even for a very short time.

# Chapter 17

Leo put his painting supplies away at Miracle Mommies and walked through the rooms to be sure everything was secure. He hadn't seen Kristin in a few days, not since he'd dropped her off the day of the ultrasound appointment. She'd given him the key code to the house so he could come and go as he pleased. But it hadn't been the same when she didn't show up when he painted.

This evening, he would see Kristin. They were babysitting the little ones so the two wedding couples could get last-minute details taken care of.

His check of the house complete, he locked up and went outside. On the porch, he pulled his coat around his neck. He could see his breath, but the cold had let up, leaving it still very chilly but not the bitter, frigid temps he disliked. The sun shone brightly on the ground, and he would have believed it was ten degrees warmer just because of it.

Pulling away from Kristin's property, an ache in his chest from missing her took him off guard. What was wrong with him? He wasn't ready for a relationship. Even if he had been, Kristin wasn't available—not with her life choices. A ready-made family would make anyone stop and think.

When he'd come in to work this morning, it was spitting snow. But the white stuff had increased gradually. By the time he got to the end of her lane, the snow had turned up a few notches. Big, fluffy flakes came down. It was beautiful, especially with Christmas Eve coming in three days.

The desire to see Kristin, to be around her and able to enjoy the snow, which she'd always loved, hit him hard. He didn't try to fight the feeling. He didn't want to. Maybe he would lean into it, like his counselor sometimes said, and come up with a plan and implement it. He started up his truck and used his phone contacts list to call Caleb.

The phone rang several times, and he was about to disconnect when Caleb's voice came on. "What're you doing calling me?" The irritation in his voice evident, Leo nearly discarded his mission.

But he'd reached out to lay the groundwork, even though he and his brother lived separately on the same property. "That's no way to greet a brother. I can imagine you've got a lot going on, so I forgive you." Preparing someone for a new idea seemed like a good idea, in order to get the best reception to it. Everyone was so busy.

"Whoever started this lunacy of getting married in barns ought to face some serious consequences."

As he drove, he took in the stark trees without their leaves that edged the road. He favored leaves, but the bare limbs were an art form all their own.

"You're at a disadvantage because your barns aren't sitting empty and all prettied up like people who use theirs for events only, all the popular, fancy venues. From what I've seen, you're in fine shape though. You sure you aren't getting cold feet?"

Those trees, the way they contrasted with the sky. Even on break, everything came to him through an artist's lens. He couldn't hold himself back anymore. Leo pulled over, got out of the truck, and reached underneath the seat where he kept his camera bag hidden. While listening, he snapped tree shots.

"It would've made a difference if Wyatt wasn't slammed with his work unexpectedly. It's his wedding day, too."

*Click. Click.* He hoped Caleb wouldn't think anything of the camera sounds, but his brothers were all used to how he worked. Leo had a knot in the pit of his stomach, which might possibly be an inkling of regret. When he asked his brothers if he could help, they had declined his offer, and he hadn't pressed them into letting him do more wedding tasks. Some might have called the emotion guilt, but he'd banned that sentiment and didn't allow it in. Not anymore.

"Relax. I'll help. But I've got a favor to ask first."

"Okay. Two of us should be able to knock it out quickly, but what's it going to cost me?"

He drove in under the arch that said Galloway Sons Farm and led up to the houses. He inhaled, warmth filling his chest. Feeling like a part of the family, even in a peripheral way, meant more to him than he wanted to admit.

"Look, grab you a cold drink, jot down everything needs done. I'll be up to the house in about thirty minutes."

"You can't sweet talk me. I know your methods. Tell me what you're wanting."

"See you in thirty minutes." Leo disconnected the call.

He pulled into the short drive of the house on the property he'd been crashing at for his short stay. Coming to a stop beside the back door, he grabbed his lunch bag from the truck and strode inside. When ideas came to him, they took over his mind like a wildfire—all-consuming and hard to contain.

Once inside, he tore through the rooms until he came to his bedroom, then dragged his luggage out from the closet. Patting down the zippered outer pockets, he found what he wanted. Even though he'd brought the basics for travel, his fingers gripped the paintbrush and looked over the paints like a kid returning to his toys he'd been separated from. He found a place to sit where he could look out the window and pulled up his photo of a tree on the camera screen to begin.

Being away from work made him appreciate the experience all the more, and if he wasn't careful, he'd get involved and wouldn't look up for hours. But he'd made a commitment to Caleb, and excitement about his plan spurred him on to making a quick start to return to later.

He took care of his brushes and sealed the paint up tight so they'd be ready for next time, then grabbed his coat and headed out. The snow fell heavier, blanketing the trees, and the landscape was breathtaking, like a Christmas movie set. The main house could have inspired actors in a musical to start singing. He stuck out his tongue, and a snowflake landed on it. How had he never noticed Indiana's beauty?

"What took you so long?" Caleb peeked out the door, and the man had to have been waiting and watching for him.

Leo went up on the porch and entered through the door Caleb held open.

Being the older brother had perks he intended to use. "Come sit down over here and lean back. I've never seen you like this. It's enough to put me off marriage, except I already wasn't a fan. Let me massage your shoulders a bit while we talk."

"No way."

"Don't knock it 'til you've tried it. I reacted the same the first couple of times, and now I get professional messages regularly. Learned a couple things I'll try on you."

Caleb's shoulders sagged, and he flopped into the chair and leaned back. Leo might have had to badger his brother into it, but he was never one to back down. His family knew it, and that helped him keep them in line.

Putting his hands on his brother's shoulders, Leo had no trouble finding tight muscles and went to work.

Caleb moaned. "Amazing."

"Here's what we're going to do. We'll get your list covered

however we have to in the next couple of days. I mean, we have money, and if we need help, we're going to use it to hire people. At the same time, we'll put my plan into play."

"Which is?"

"Remember when we were little and Gram and Gramps took us on a sleigh ride around our woods every year, or were you too little? They played Christmas carols and hymns." By thinking way back, before he'd ever thought about a line of work or gotten into it with Dad, he tapped into wonderful memories.

"Of course. It was one of the highlights of my childhood."

"Mine too. Well, I've made some calls, and we're going to bring it back this year, only bigger and better."

"Wait, we've got the weddings."

"Trust me on this. I've found the contact to make it all happen tomorrow night. It'll be fun. I'm going to go big and invite the community in."

"Are you nuts?"

"We need it. Everybody could use some fun. It's been a year and a half for the record books. There's Kayla's situation. I can't even bring myself to say the word 'addict.' We lost Dad. Now Kayla's back. Two weddings. Kristin's having triplets. Not that she's in the family."

Caleb sat up. "Watch yourself with Kristin, big brother."

Leo's temper threatened to flare up. He stopped the message and clenched his hands into fists. "She's my best friend's kid sister. We're friends." Then why was he getting so worked up when Caleb implied it was more?

"I know you. She's a good kid and she's been through some really tough times."

"That's not her fault."

"This isn't about her. It's about you. I see a guy who's charted his course, been a free spirit his whole life. Also, he has a big heart, the one who adopted the stray animals around the farm that people dropped off. You're a rock, Leo. You like fixer-uppers, which goes for houses, animals, and people. A nice single gal with triplets isn't something an artist and confirmed bachelor can fix."

"You've got it all wrong." But hadn't he been thinking something similar, that he needed to tread lightly?

"Okay… There is something that needs done, which is the provision of Dad's will. It says we all have to contribute to keeping up the farm in some meaningful way."

"I'm not ready to give details yet, but I've got something in mind." Maybe that little painting could be the start of something more.

Caleb stood up and got his list. "Now let's get some things marked off before it's babysitting time."

He headed out to the barn, and Leo followed.

He felt gutted by what Caleb said associated with Kristin but shouldn't be. Everything he'd said was true. So why the knot in the pit of his stomach when he thought of Kristin on her own?

# Chapter 18

Kristin looked around the huge living room at the Galloway homestead. Toys were strewn everywhere. Farm animals had been tossed from their plastic barn into a heap. A doll with few clothes on and its head turned around wrong lay by a miniature baby bed with stuffed animals stretched out under the sheets.

When Leo's brothers and their fiancées had asked them to watch the children, she hadn't hesitated. Leo had held back, but eventually he'd agreed.

Leo let out a whinny from down on the floor where he was on his hands and knees and pretended to gallop with Ella riding on his back. As a result of the little girl getting scared and screaming in his ear when he went fast, he had slowed his pace down to a crawl.

From her seat on the sofa, she paused her crocheting and called over to them. "Does the horsey need a drink?"

He stopped and gazed at her with those brown eyes. "That sounds great."

"Me. Me," the three toddlers joined in.

With exaggerated motions, Leo assisted Ella in getting down from his back.

"Let me help this cowgirl dismount. Be careful getting out of the saddle, honey."

The kids toddled into the kitchen, and Leo loosely put his arm around Kristin's shoulder as they walked in together. She snuggled in. "You're great with them, you know that?"

"I don't know much about this. But I'll have to take your word for it. I'm having fun."

She went to the refrigerator, opened the door, and he separated from her to go sit at the table. Every part of her wanted him back next to her.

*Focus, Kristin.* She concentrated on getting the sippy cups with milk Sierra had measured out perfectly for their before-bed routine. As they giggled and shared their own little times, she took a seat by Leo.

"Wonder what it'll be like with my three."

His open, carefree expression slipped into hiding. "You'll be amazing, no matter what."

So why the long face, she wanted to ask. "Thanks for saying that. I hope so. But these guys are grown-ups compared to newborns. They even hold their own cups."

A green sippy cup bounced onto the table and sailed off onto the floor. He smiled and got up, the sparkle in his eyes returning.

"You spoke too soon." He stooped down, retrieved the cup, and returned it to Max.

"Tan too!"

Leo scrubbed his hand on the boy's head for a few seconds. "You're welcome, young man."

They got them down and headed back into the living room. "You sure the horsey is okay with putting them to bed?"

"I wouldn't have volunteered if I didn't think so."

"You're hard to figure out."

"I didn't say I didn't like kids."

That was true. He guided her to the sofa, and she plopped down, happy for the comfortable seat. The room seemed decorated with sweet little faces, and she inhaled a breath of the pine scent. Must be a spray, since they had an artificial tree up in the far corner.

At least she'd get plenty of practice with kids if she hung out with Leo—while he was here in Fair Creek anyway. For a guy who wasn't interested in having kids, he was exceptionally good with them.

Ella went to a small plate of treats on a table with a Christmas-themed cloth. She held up a spongy Christmas tree that was made of sugar. "Twee," she said.

Leo smiled. "Yum." Ella popped it in her mouth. Kristin shuddered inwardly and how sweets might impact her, especially before bed. But Leo had enough insecurities about his experiences with children and she wasn't going to add to them.

The kids hadn't shed a tear. Actually, maybe they had more fun when no one was parenting them by limiting their intake of sweets and tempting them with carrots.

But it was time to put them to bed, for real. Kristin picked up the list Annie and Sierra had written, carefully reading their notes on recreating the steps they used to put the little ones to bed. Fortunately, both women were heavy on reading, just like her. The children's books stacked on the table had sing-song titles, like a lullaby but using only words, and there were images of sleeping babies tucked into baskets.

She would give Leo a nudge. Kristin used her best, soothing voice. "Kids, it's time to read."

Drew toddled his way to a shelf overflowing with books and brought one to Leo.

"Monsters?" Leo quirked an eyebrow and glanced at Kristin, then back at Drew. "Sure, buddy." He came and sat on the sofa with her, and the little boy followed and stood beside his knee.

Adorable. Who wouldn't swoon over a man who listened to an eighteen-month-old? Max walked over and so did Ella, and dropped a board book featuring dolls as she went. They clustered around Leo and the bright, animated monster book. Of course, girls would love monsters, too, especially if the boys did.

Ella climbed onto her lap, and Kristin leaned her head on Leo's shoulder so they were snuggled close. She inhaled the little-girl scent, appreciating the warm, muscled arm by her side all the more. Leo reached up and dimmed the lamp, and the tree lights put a colorful glow on their little group. Perfect.

What would this be like when she had her own little ones?

Leo began reading. He roared on each page the monster appeared. It was a realistic, gruff sound, and the kids giggled and Ella screamed once. Several pages in, the little boys started adding their growls to Leo's. Ella shrieked.

Kristin hugged the little girl tight. "You're safe, sweetie."

What would it be like if Leo stayed with her after the babies were born? Could she have the family she'd always dreamed of?

He said that's not what he wanted, so she had to take him at his word.

He sure was good with kids though.

Kristin checked her watch. Five minutes past when the lights were supposed to be out. Drew jumped off the sofa and ran around growling. The kids seemed more wound up than ever. Max joined his cousin, chasing around the coffee table. Now she knew why its edges were all plastered with tape.

Leo left the sofa and guided each boy by the shoulder back to the sofa and read another page.

Kristin took out the book from the table that had a teddy bear family being tucked in by the stuffed mother bear and thumbed through the pages for Ella. These stories would have been more appropriate to prepare for sleep.

Leo looked up with the biggest grin on his face.

Her heart melted. "Let's thank your uncle for reading to you."

They hugged Leo and clapped.

It was a special night, and being with Leo was more important than getting to bed on time. They weren't crying for their parents or anything, so that was good.

He may have sensed she was getting concerned. "Kids, this is a longer book than I thought. Why don't we stop, and we can read the rest in the morning. It's bedtime." He started to close the book.

A hand reached into the book's pages. "No." Drew wasn't defiant exactly, just determined. Leo resumed reading, in a subdued tone, without one roar.

Soon it was ten minutes past bedtime, and everyone looked droopy, including Leo. He closed the book and put it on the side table. "I'm so glad you chose this book, and I love it too, but it's bedtime."

Drew started to cry. Max and Ella followed his lead. Leo looked up at Kristin and shrugged his shoulders. "What do I do now?" he mouthed.

She stood and went to the boys and patted Drew's back. "It's okay, honey. We're all tired. Let's get you into your own bed." When Leo saw how the little boy calmed down, he took the same approach with Max.

By the time they were all in fresh diapers, into pajamas, and settled in their beds on their backs, as Kristin's instructions said to do, it was forty-five minutes past their bedtime. Each dropped off to sleep without a peep.

Kristin's feet were rooted to the floor, she was so drawn to their peaceful faces as they slept. Leo seemed in no hurry to move either.

He leaned over and kissed her cheek. "Just think, you'll be doing these same routines with your little ones. And I won't be there riling them up, either, so it'll be easier."

She stayed close next to him, not daring to look into his eyes, afraid of what might be missing from his gaze. "That's where you're wrong. I'd give anything for them to have a wonderful man like you in their life, monster books at bedtime and all."

He cupped her chin in his hand and gazed into her eyes, speaking in hushed tones. "It's so nice to hear you say that. But we both know there's so much more to caring for children. When I'm working, my mind's far away. A lot of times, I'm actually in another physical place."

She wasn't going to try to persuade him, and she certainly wouldn't beg. She kept her gaze locked with his, keeping her voice low. "No parent can be with them every minute. Maybe you're convinced you wouldn't be a good dad because you've got an unrealistic view, Leo. Two adults working together gives them a better chance, but there will always be gaps."

They were inches apart, and he brushed his lips across hers. "You make me want to believe. Tonight's been special, just the two of us. Well, plus three little ones."

She didn't know where any of this would lead, but when he kissed her for real, she leaned in, and the sweetness sent warmth through her. Her arms went around his neck, and he deepened the kiss. They fit together, and when she inhaled his woodsy scent, he felt like home.

He pulled away too soon and gazed into her eyes. The gold

specks in his dark-brown ones reached out to her. "I don't want to make promises I can't keep."

She patted her stomach. "There's no commitment. They are my responsibility, and we'll be fine, God willing."

How could she trust him when her relationship with Craig had started out with such promise? Maybe Leo's hesitation was a sign they shouldn't be together. She prayed for wisdom, to know what to do.

He reached out and touched her hand.

She clasped on, laced their fingers together, and they headed out of Drew and Ella's bedroom where Max always had a place, pulling the door behind them, except for a slight opening, as the instructions specified. All their micromanaging seemed silly.

For her own babies, she'd have to create her own instructions. Could she do it? Did she want to by herself? There really wasn't any other choice. *You won't be alone.* God seemed to have put the words in her mind.

They were partway down the hallway when Leo smiled. "Where were you for a minute, off somewhere else? How about popcorn and a movie?"

They entered the kitchen, and he made his way to the counter where he managed to locate the air popper. It struck her as such a guy thing to do, and she smiled. She found herself humming as he gave her the job of adding the butter, and her knuckles grazed his. "Let's not tell the parents when we got them to bed, okay? Think they'll be upset?"

"No. Just the way we didn't tell our own parents everything.

I see now that it was a mistake to let those little cuties get me involved in that monster story."

She giggled, tugging his hat off and placing it on a barstool. His dark lashes were longer than she'd remembered. Butterflies danced in her stomach. "That's forty-five minutes I could have spent alone with you that I'll never get back."

His eyes opened wide, and she noticed he gave extra focus while the popper dumped the popped corn into a huge bowl. Kristin reached for the two serving bowls left on the counter, and Leo placed his hand on hers. "Leave those. Let's share."

Warmth shot up Kristin's arm. Her mouth went dry.

Just for tonight, she would forget about everything but Leo.

He led her through the living room, littered with toys, down the hallway into a den next to the kids' bedroom. "I don't trust baby monitors. With the door cracked open, we'll hear them if they need anything."

How could she let this man go? "You sure know how to sweet talk a girl. An expectant mom anyway."

Lines crossed his forehead. "That's not what I'm going for here."

His eyes didn't have their sparkle, and a shadow crossed his face. "Have some popcorn. I've chosen my favorite Christmas movie."

Kristin grabbed some popcorn. "What's that romcom, I forget the name of it?"

Taking a fistful of popcorn, he held it up toward his mouth. "Nope." He emptied his popcorn into his mouth.

"You're going to make me guess?"

"Yes, although I'm setting you up for failure."

There had to be a way for her to outsmart him. While she racked her brain, she tossed a piece of popcorn at him. "You underestimate me, something people have done all my life, to their peril."

He managed to catch the popcorn in his mouth. Those lips. Oh why didn't he just kiss her already? Who cared about a stupid movie anyway.

He reached into the bowl for more popcorn, placing their faces just inches apart. "You're pretty sure of yourself there. But you have no clue. Tell you what, if you're wrong, I get to finish that kiss we started earlier."

Her breath caught in her throat, and she came closer to look deep into his eyes. "You really know how to pressure somebody." She wanted to lose but had to compete since she'd always played to win. Her voice came out all whispery. "It's the one where the whole town comes together in the end, isn't it?"

"Close. You're getting warmer." His grin was more like a smug smile.

"There's the old one with that little girl and Santa."

"Nope. You're getting colder. I'll put you out of your misery. It's an animated Christmas story most people haven't heard of."

She smacked her hand on her jeans in mock alarm. "Are you kidding me?"

When he came in for the kiss, she didn't move, not until their lips met. He was firm and warm, tasting of butter threaded through with a hint of salt.

Kristin's toes curled, and she couldn't remember a kiss ever being so fine. Leo filled her mind and her senses. The boy she'd known merged with the man he'd become.

When he finally ended the kiss, she inhaled a deep breath.

He smiled, the sparkle back in his eyes. "Rusty Shultz was a genius. Ready to watch with me?"

"Who's Rusty Shultz?"

"The guy who made the animated movie we're going to watch."

She wanted to know what that kiss was all about but suspected asking would make it like so many special moments. If over-analyzed, they were ruined. She'd learned that the hard way.

The movie didn't hold her attention when Leo's hand on hers was all she could think of. Before the movie was halfway over, the sounds of car doors opening and closing, followed by voices, filtered into the room. Kristin hopped up and Leo did, too.

"Didn't mean to startle you," Caleb said

As if she was in another world, Kristin listened to Leo explain how the kids had gone down to bed perfectly. All was good. The parents would never know.

On his drive to take her home, they held hands all the way, neither seeming to have it in them to put into words the evening they'd shared.

He walked her to her door, gave her a peck on the cheek.

Filled with disappointment, for no real reason, she watched him leave, then closed her door behind him, then leaned on it and sank to the floor.

What had she done? Was she falling for a man she knew she couldn't have?

The heart knew what it knew. God had carried her this far. He'd help her to face whatever came next. She'd just have to believe he meant it all for good, as scripture said.

# Chapter 19

Leo walked outside among the barns at Galloway Sons Farm, his fur-lined jacket protecting him from the chilly air. The temperatures were just right, cold enough to signal Christmastime and a winter wonderland, yet not freezing and dangerous for fingers and toes. He made sure the helpers Caleb had hired for the night had the horses on a rotation and were well cared for. The sleighs had been checked for safety.

He looked up at the fields flowing with Fair Creek townspeople making their way back from the far field where his family's private air strip had made the perfect surface for a little Christmas parade. Some of the farmers had brought ponies and seated the older kids up in the wagons and let them toss candy.

He checked that a half door of the barn was open and Girl Scouts from a Fair Creek troop handed out free hot apple cider or hot chocolate. The warm drinks gave off steam into the cold air. Sierra had concocted dozens of her famous varieties of cookies. Leo made a mental note to catch a whiff of molasses crinkles, snickerdoodles, and brownies. But he needed to do something else first.

"How's your party going, cowboy?" That voice made his heart sing. Leo swung the yellow lantern light toward the sound and almost didn't recognize Kristin. She was bundled in a quilted cream coat that reached below her knees with a bright-red knitted cap pulled down over her hair, and those unmistakable eyes like a darkening night sky were all that clued him in.

He leaned over toward her. "My celebration just started."

"Why?"

"Because I schemed to create this entire event just to snuggle with you in the sleigh."

Her eyes grew wide and the already rosy color of her cheeks darkened, like terra cotta clay pots he'd painted in Italy. "You make that sound delicious, decadent even."

He lifted an eyebrow her way, then turned as a sleigh pulled up to the barn, jam-packed with five adults and three children. Leo reached for Kristin's hand and led her there. "Come on. I'm pretty sure I know who that is."

Caleb and Annie, Wyatt and Sierra, as well as Kayla, were laughing as they unwrapped their arms from around one another and their four young charges climbed off laps as they deboarded.

Leo went up to Wyatt, whose arms surrounded Max. He patted the little boy's head. "Hey, Maxie! Would you and your dad oversee things while we go on a ride by ourselves?" He addressed Wyatt. "The refreshments are under control, and all is running smoothly."

Wyatt put on a fake frown, although the light from the barn showed his eyes twinkled. "You thinking about kidnapping Kristin or something?"

Kristin waved the hand that wasn't in his. "I'm a willing captive!"

Leo smiled and his heart warmed at Max and the others' eyes peeping out of their bright-red snowsuit hoods, all the cousins matching, as they gurgled and jabbered at the hubbub around them.

Chloe grinned, wearing a quilted coat that matched Kristin's, except it was red with a faux fur white hat with knitted string having fur clumps on the ends that tied under her chin. A banner that said "Birthday Girl" stretched from her shoulder to her waist.

"Hope you're having a great early birthday." When he'd been told her birthday would be Christmas Eve, when the weddings would take place, he'd combined her celebration with the Christmas party.

She gave him a huge grin. "I almost feel bad, I'm getting so many extra presents with all these people. I'll take one of them. Come here, Max." The little boy looked at her, wide-eyed. "Come see the horsey."

Leo and Kristin climbed into the waiting sleigh.

Kristin laughed as the kids left. "Well, at least they get the chance to see a real horse, not ride on their uncle's back only."

The Christmas music piped out from the barn played "Joy to the World" into the night. As they pulled away, the "Sleigh Ride" song that had the sound of a horse whinny came on.

They positioned themselves on the seat, and Leo reached behind them and grabbed a blanket and covered their laps.

She leaned in. "What made you think of doing this?"

"You. You give me ideas I've never had before. An appreciation for how I was raised and for the great memories. And there were some. I've let the remarks about my career choices overshadow everything else. My brothers may not have been like me, but if they judged me, I was equally responsible for judging them. I thought they had no vision of their futures, but of course they did, and they left, too. I really couldn't understand them coming back here, and Dad's will, the provisions of which he required us to keep secret, bringing me back here seemed to prove I should only come if forced. But now I see that maybe what I was missing was being grounded in tradition and always looking for the latest thrill or the biggest commission wasn't satisfying."

He leaned down and his lips met hers, all his affection for her poured into their connection. Warmth filled him, and when she moaned and reached her arms around his neck, she tasted of cinnamon and cider. He was lost in their kiss when the horse pulled in next to the barn.

Scrambling up, they stayed arm in arm as they climbed out of the sleigh. He took her hand while helping her down. "Come over here. I'd like to show you something." He led her to a framed piece of art hanging on a wall by itself. "This is a preliminary painting because I wouldn't have my finished one out here in the elements." The sun shone over the image of Miracle Mommies House. Wheat in the fields was a burnished gold.

"You did this for me, when I've been demanding so much of you?"

"I'm glad you like it. Art is how I process life and spending time at Miracle Mommies made me want to create a memory of it."

"You're on a break to relax, and you make something like this? You're married to your work and art is your baby."

"I don't agree. Your dedication to MM House inspires me. I've asked God to give me more meaning, to simplify my life so I'm not so stressed. I was thinking about that lately and an internal message or something responded, 'You've gotten your answer. I'm just waiting for you to see that simplifying your life means focusing on others.'"

"My path isn't going to be anyone else's. I do sometimes think that life has multiple dimensions and we're meant to appreciate them all. Sounds like your work is spiritual for you."

He'd have to think about that. They wandered over to a Christmas tree. The tree had all cream-colored cloth angels.

Kristin stepped closer and smiled. "Someone hung baby booties in among the branches!" She reached out and found three. "Everyone is supporting me. Maybe I really can do this."

"I know you will."

"These two are wearing me out." Kayla brought the twins over. She carried them so their hands and feet were sticking out level to the ground, as if they were flying in the air. "These two are wearing me out." She had the biggest grin on her face.

"Down."

"Drew, do you promise not to run from me? Mommy needs to know where you are."

Leo patted his sister's shoulder. "Kayla, I can understand how you'd worry, but this is a friendly crowd. Nothing will happen to them because if they got away from you, one of your friends and neighbors would just collect them and bring them back. Besides, Chloe watches them like they are her favorites, because they are."

Kayla exhaled and her frown left as her grip on her children eased. "That time I ran away from home, I had only walked down the street when someone asked what I was doing, listened to me, and brought me back."

Dad had known what he was doing by bringing Leo back here. They had made their peace before Dad died. But being at Galloway Sons Farm with his brothers had brought to light that he didn't have the companionship that he saw his brothers had, and what their parents exemplified.

Was he meant to have someone by his side? Things were moving quickly, and he wasn't sure about anything he'd believed before. He couldn't imagine life without Kristin in it.

# Chapter 20

"Don't believe I've ever seen a pink cowboy hat. That's the perfect touch for a Western wedding." Leo moved his chair closer to Kristin's and draped his arm around her shoulders.

She snuggled into his warmth. They'd brought in overhead heaters to fight the chilly air inside the barn. "Thanks. It's made of fur felt, nice and soft. I'm so glad we can sit together and you don't have to be up front."

"There's no place I'd rather be than right here with you."

"If I didn't know better, I say you're smooth talking me, cowboy."

"Never. But it's a plus I've got a big family to share the work tonight." Earlier, Leo had helped outside with parking cars, since they wanted to greet their guests personally. Leo wasn't in the tiny wedding party.

From where she sat on the Galloway side of the wedding party, the decorations seemed to be a combination of green garland strung along the wall creatively arranged with red bandanas. A huge, rustic wooden cross with a piece of red cloth over it stood where the vows were going to be taken.

She squeezed his arm. "I've never been to a double wedding ceremony."

"Not sure how it's going to go. I helped with some of the music though. That's an acoustic violin you're listening to."

She turned around to look at where some kind of country sounds were coming from. "That's unique. I'm impressed."

"I couldn't do anything halfway, so I've got another small group with an electric violinist playing folk music, I think they said it was."

"You continue to surprise me. I had no idea."

"I didn't have much of an idea either, so we'll see how it goes." He leaned in and spoke quietly next to her ear. "There's Ted and my Aunt Elizabeth."

Kristin casually peeked over his shoulder at the man from Delaney's the other day. "They're a handsome couple." The older man wore Western styling that was all black. The woman wore blue, including a cowboy hat like here. Both had on cowboy boots.

Leo tilted his head toward another woman who entered without any escort. "Do you know who that is??

"Trudy. She styles everybody's hair."

"What's she doing here? They said the ceremony's family-only.

She ran her finger through her curls she'd had done for the occasion. "Trudy told me that Sierra and Annie made her an honorary family member so she can be on hand, in case they have a hair malfunction."

He laughed.

"Is this seat taken?" Standing beside Leo, a man she didn't recognize pointed to the empty chair on the other side of him.

Leo stood and hugged the tall cowboy who resembled him, and quietly spoke a greeting. "Nice to see you could fit this into your agenda, Gage. Always said you'd be late for your own funeral."

The man's posture stiffened, and he pulled away. "Had to really pull some strings to get away. Sorry but weddings are a dime a dozen."

If Leo was bothered by the exchange, he didn't let on. The smile didn't leave his face as the two men took their seats side by side.

She'd never known the third brother, Gage, who was under Leo in the birth order. But Gage had the reputation of being the most complex of them all. A top reporter and editor for a national communications conglomerate, stories he'd contributed to with his name on them were the talk of Fair Creek.

The bouncy music stopped and, up in front, Wyatt came in from the side and sat down in a seat that had a microphone placed. His guitar music changed the tone and helped Kristin to calm. She had no reason to be nervous, but the tension among her friends had rubbed off on her. He had a nice singing voice and wasn't playing a traditional love song. Sierra had mentioned that he'd let her choose. As his fingers strummed the strings of his guitar, sweet sounds filled the air, and the slightly melancholy tune seemed sentimental, just right for such a night.

Little Chloe came in looking so grown up as the first bridesmaid, and others followed. Her smile seemed to radiate through her whole body, and the look of adoration she gave Caleb said it all.

When Caleb went to the front and stood, he had a small, pleasant smile on his face, and his eyes seemed to sparkle, which she noticed even from this distance. Their vows would be exchanged in front of family. Afterward, they had invited everyone in town for the celebration.

The wedding music began in earnest, coming through with more intensity, and bringing her total attention to the occasion. Everything was set for the two brides to enter.

She squeezed Leo's hand and would have guaranteed that her heart swelled as Kayla came into view with Drew and Ella. After a chaotic rehearsal, they'd opted to let their mother walk in front of her little ones to keep them on task, if that were possible. But it also showed everyone how well she was doing and that she had conquered her addictions. Max tagged along, with a red-and-black flannel pillow holding two wedding rings attached with a bow. All were dressed like little wranglers, even Ella.

Kayla was the only blond in the Galloway family and stood

out among her dark-haired brothers. She had requested to live in one of the homes on the property, since Caleb and Annie would be living in the main house, so the little cousins would be raised close together. Sleepovers and breakfasts and all the other things they had done during Kayla's absence were already on the docket.

Drew pulled a small red wagon full of daisies sourced from local farms, they'd been told, and Ella dropped them along as they went. Before they gave him the wagon, he'd used a basket and had gone running and throwing petals everywhere, according to Annie. Midway down the aisle, he sat down with a handful of flowers and studied them, and Chloe left her place and guided him to what he was supposed to do.

The quartet of mom and twins plus their cousin reached the primitive altar, and Drew dropped the wagon handle and ran to Kayla. Ella followed, and their mom stooped down and gathered both of them into her arms. A collective sigh from all those in attendance seemed to go up. Max marched up to where Wyatt and Caleb stood together and gave his dad the pillow.

Both brides had lost their fathers years ago, and the two women cousins stood at the back of the room arm in arm. Everyone stood as they proceeded forward, showing a strong similarity to one another in stature. Both wore their hair swept away from their faces. Their hair shade clearly set them apart, with Sierra's red hair taking on a rich, auburn hue in the dimly-lit barn, her pale skin nearly translucent, the freckles peeking out across the bridge of her nose adding the perfect touch. Annie's blonde hair gave her an angelic appearance, and her face had the lightest tan glow. She wore deep-rose lipstick that accentuated her full lips and deep-blue eyes.

Pastor Frond spoke from the passage about Ruth and Naomi about where you go I'll go. Kristin's eyes became unexpectedly misty. She'd always loved that scripture, except things hadn't worked out that way for her. She gave a quick touch to her stomach. It would be nice to know what her future held, or at least who her future would be with. God would be with her, and her three precious bundles were going to be with her, whatever came next. She shot up a prayer the Lord would keep them healthy and strong. The risks were great for multiples. She mentally breathed out the words. A thought of her ex flitted through her mind. Her babies' father couldn't be there for them. But her time spent with Leo had shown her that there were good men out there. Surely, God would provide for all their needs as He always did.

She sneaked a sideways glance at Leo. His dark-brown eyes under his cowboy hat were intense, even for him, as he studied the ceremony. He caught her eyes in a steady gaze that seemed to hold a promise. But he'd said his art was everything to him, and she believed him. Maybe God had placed him here for a short time to shore her up and give her hope.

Or was Leo undergoing a shift in thinking? Could a guy his age, or of any age, have a change of heart that was that drastic? Did she want him to?

"To have and to hold, until death do us part." She swallowed the lump in her throat. Both couples stood and faced one another, repeating the preacher's words. A shiver went down her spine when Caleb recited his vows to Annie, saying what her helping with the babies meant to him. She vowed to try to be neater, and the audience chuckled, and so did her husband-to-be. The pastor advised to "promise to appreciate the ways you are different, remembering how you are the same, and never forget you are created by God. Treasure what you two can be together, with God's blessing."

Part of Wyatt's vows said, "to be there for you and to be your helpmate that we will raise our son together." Sierra was going to adopt Max, since his mother died so soon after he was born.

The exchanges resonated so much that she had trouble concentrating on what the others said in their vows. What would it be like to have someone pledge to spend the rest of their lives together and for him to express such adoration? Given her past, it seemed impossible and even felt greedy. She grazed her hand along her belly again. Could anyone even dare to wish for more than one miracle in a lifetime, when she had already had three?

"You may kiss the bride," the pastor said. Caleb kissed Annie with enthusiasm and dipped her down to some laughs from onlookers. Wyatt put his hands on either side of Sierra's face and kissed her with almost reverence, their lips touching so slightly at first that Kristin felt a flutter in her stomach as they then deepened their kiss. Then Wyatt lifted his bride slightly above the ground and spun her around once.

The pastor addressed the audience. "Let me introduce Mr. and Mrs. Galloway, times two."

# Chapter 21

An area of the barn had been roped off for the reception. Leo sat at a round table next to Kristin, wishing the evening would end. Yellow light radiated from the lantern that decorated the center of the table, and pulled pork sandwiches, cowboy chili, and cowboy fare had been delicious. Sierra's black raspberry pies in lieu of wedding cake had hit the spot, and an army of volunteers had even churned the ice cream to make it ala mode.

"I don't think I've ever experienced line dancing before."

Kristin started to answer, and loud music started again, joined by someone shouting out the steps into a microphone.

Kristin giggled and shouted over the din. "You haven't missed much. I'm fairly athletic, played sports all through school. It took me less than one song and I knew it wasn't for me." She shrugged.

"When you know, you know."

He made a show of feeling around the dimly-lit table until he found Kristin's hand where it rested on the table.

He covered her hand with his. "We're a match made in heaven," he teased. "So glad you aren't dragging me out there."

She laced her fingers in between his. "That's the key to your heart, huh? Rejecting line dancing? I've wondered."

"Why aren't you on the dance floor?"

Leo stared up into the dark. "Not you still here, Gage? I've lost all respect for you."

A woman who looked familiar stepped close to the table. "Come on, Kristin. You're missing all the fun."

Kristin looked at him, and he almost thought she was going to throw him under the bus and say yes. "Well, Bree, I—"

"Hi, guys. Hope you're enjoying the party." Kayla stepped close to the table. "Oh, didn't mean to interrupt."

The music started up again, and Bree said, "That's 'Scootin' and Bootin',' my favorite." The two of them hurried away.

Good. It was getting crowded over here, Leo thought. His sister stood next to the table, seeming a little stiff all by herself, and awkwardly shifted from one foot to the other. He wondered how she was working back into the community.

"Kayla, I've been wanting to chat with you. Do you have time to join us?"

She didn't move forward, just looked at Kristin. "Are you sure you're okay if I do?"

Kristin nodded her approval, and Leo pointed to the seat on

the other side of him. Kayla's demeanor changed, and she seemed more at ease after coming over and sitting down.

"Hey, Leo."

Now that she was here, he wasn't sure how to start. "You, Ella, and Drew did great earlier at the ceremony, by the way."

She gave him a half smile, her forehead almost in a frown, and picked up the leather string on the table that held the napkin together. "Oh, Aunt Elizabeth is babysitting them. They're wiped. Things are perfect. We've set up a schedule, Caleb and Annie and me, sort of like visitation but nothing that formal or rigid. They're taking the twins and Max to the petting zoo soon, actually."

They looked at each other. Kristin took a sip of water from a mason jar with twine around the edge. "That's great. I loved the little zoo when I was young. You mean the one in Poppyville, the next town over, right?"

Kayla nodded. "That's right." She looked so young, so vulnerable. He was more than a decade older.

*Form words. You can do it.*

"I've heard— I mean, I've read—" Kayla's green eyes bore into his, and her hands twisted the leather string. He stumbled on. "It can't be easy, what you've been through. What can I do to help?"

It was dark, but he thought her eyes looked shiny. Were those unshed tears? "That's really, really nice of you to ask. Not that many people are talking to me. I feel like they're waiting for me to fail. Maybe I'm waiting on myself to fail."

*Don't correct what she says.* "Addiction isn't an easy thing. I'm not going to say the word 'fail.' I hope you've got people you can call, if you need to."

She didn't say anything. Her eyes were too beautiful to look so sad.

"What I'm saying is, I will be a person. You know, my issues, let's say, haven't been as public as yours, but I'm not always doing so great either."

"Come on, big brother. I'm not buying that."

He glanced over at Kristin, not sure if he wanted to have this conversation and whether it should be in her presence. She nodded, and her eyes seemed to convey to go ahead.

"I'm just saying that you had your writing, and I had my art." She used to write and to be on the school newspaper and write stories. That was received about as well as his art. "It made us the odd ones out in this family. I worry about failure too. I guess I think our parents, in some ways, failed us. I'm not fighting addiction, like you are. But I've fought having a life with a family. What if I failed them? I don't admit that. I just say I don't want a family. But I really don't think I could do it well."

Kayla put her hand on his shoulder, then removed it. "I know that's not true. Just in the short time I've been here, I can see you're good with kids."

"Well, thank you for the vote of confidence. It just goes so much deeper than that."

"Yeah, I know what you mean. I'll be fighting this addiction all my life. It's not over."

"I believe in you. You can do it. I just don't want you to be isolated. Don't let people get you down."

Kristin leaned in. "Kayla, we want you to stay clean. All of us do. And if we don't know how to help, please tell us what you need, okay?"

Kayla nodded. "Look, thanks for this. I do feel isolated. It goes with the territory for moms of young children. But this is different. It's like people think addiction's contagious. Or maybe they don't know what to say, so they say nothing. Anyway, I'm glad you said something."

Kayla got up, and as she walked away, maybe he imagined it, but she didn't look quite so stiff and uncertain. Leo exhaled. "That didn't go too badly, did it?"

Kristin put her arm around him. "You did amazing. The door's open now, and that's what is important. Communication."

"Hey, unless you're going to have a change of heart and go cut a rug out there, I'd like to show you something."

She stood. "Let's go."

Leo took her hand and led her toward another part of the barn. They came to the stage area, and the D.J. spoke. "We're going to shift gears here, folks. By the way, congratulations to Caleb and Annie and Wyatt and Sierra. This next song is for those of you who want to hold your honey close."

Willie Nelson singing "You Were Always on My Mind" filled the room.

Leo stopped and stood close to Kristin, nuzzling her ear as he spoke. "This is more like it. May I have this dance?"

"I thought you'd never ask."

They moved together toward the edge of the dance floor and

joined dozens more couples who were already swaying to the music.

Kristin kept a slight distance between them as they danced. Maybe she really didn't care about him as much as he cared for her? But as the lyrics and music flowed, the somewhat stiff way she held herself disappeared. By the time another song came on that was slow and had a country crooner longing for love, she was snuggled in close. The scent of her hair and the smoothness of her hand in his had him closing his eyes and savoring her nearness.

"Maybe weddings aren't all bad," he murmured in her ear.

Her voice dreamy and low, she answered, "You won't get any argument from me."

The music picked up, and he reluctantly pulled away from dancing. "I'd still like to show you something."

They strolled through the vast building, until he brought her to a secluded area of the barn where he'd hung the small art he'd made of the winter trees.

Letting the art speak for itself, he showed her his small canvas of the trees he'd painted of Indiana. He liked studying her while she looked at the piece. She let go of his hand and went closer.

It felt like several minutes but was likely only many seconds while he waited for her response to his art work. When she finished, she turned, came back to where he was, and hugged him. "I just love your art, Leo Galloway, and I am falling in love with you."

He leaned down toward her upturned face and when his lips

brushed hers, the sweetness of raspberries and punch mixed with warmth and softness all tasted a lot like hope.

"I'm afraid I've kept you up past your bedtime, Kristin."

She smiled and nodded.

"There's something else. I've kept this hush-hush. The lawyers actually said we had to. But I'm here because Dad's will requires all of us to do something to help keep the farm going. I want my offering to be art of the area. I mean, I don't think I'll become a farmer anytime soon."

The corners of her lips turned up slightly, as if she couldn't quite believe him. "Really? Does this mean you'll stay around the farm longer than you'd planned?"

"Would that be a problem?"

# Chapter 22

Kristin's eyes were still closed, her head resting on her pillow, when the sound of toenails clicking on her hardwood floors came to her. Then silence. She opened her eyes and stared into deep-brown eyes. "Merry Christmas, Bandit."

The dog's warm, rough tongue licked her hand as her thank you. Over and over. "Okay, that's enough. You're welcome."

Kristin patted the dog's head a few times, then bounded out of bed. "Let me give you your gift. I'm heading over to the Galloways' this morning." Leo had told her to be sure to get there early.

She padded barefoot into the other room to the fireplace mantel. A red stocking she'd crocheted and had stitched "Bandit" on with green yarn hung there all by itself. Well, next year there would be four stockings. She might have to buy that many.

She blinked and stared at the lone stocking one more time. Then she pulled it down, it's solid yarn feeling thick between her fingers. She pulled out the package of chew sticks inside and broke it open.

She gave one to Bandit, who went over to the corner of the room and laid down to get comfortable while she chewed. "I'm not going to take it from you, silly."

The double weddings had been so special. At the end of the evening, Leo invited her to come spend Christmas morning with his family. This was an odd year, with everything that happened, and for some reason she hadn't made Christmas plans, so she was free and said yes. Then she'd come home last night and laid out everything she was going to wear today.

Kristin went to the chair where she'd spread out her red shirt and favorite jeans. Bandit finished her treat and came in for more.

In record time, she'd fed Bandit, gotten herself ready, and headed for the door, where Bandit stood. Kristin fought the urge to bring her, but there was no way to know what she'd find at the Galloways, with all the kids and couples.

In the end, Bandit bolted out to run, looking happy, so Kristin didn't felt good about leaving her.

Within half an hour, she was pulling up to the farm, where she parked and exited the car. On her way up to the porch, the door opened, and Leo peeked out. "Everyone's asleep," he said. "Come on in."

Kristin smiled. "Can't blame them. Last night's wedding was

epic and they're worn out."

"Let me take your coat. I'm actually happy things turned out this way. Now I'll have you all to myself."

He gave her a quick hug, and she reached on tiptoes to give him a peck on the cheek.

"I like how you think."

Leo went to the counter and showed her homemade French bread in a cellophane bag decorated with green holly leaves and red berries and raspberries divided into small bowls with snowflakes on them. "We can feast on this until the others get up. Sierra brought some of her legendary coffee cake, too."

She went over and stood by him, slipping her arm around his waist. "Being with you always makes me feel special."

"You deserve to be spoiled. Speaking of which, there's a little heated porch area with lots of windows I'd like to take you to. We'll eat in there." The assorted items had been arranged on a silver tray and he reached for its handles to bring it with them.

Kristin smiled. "You've thought of everything."

He led the way and she followed. "It's logical we're the only ones awake, since the babies don't know it's Christmas, and everyone went to bed late. Chloe knows what it's all about, but she's exhausted after her wedding adventures."

Kristin had learned last night that the newlyweds wouldn't take their honeymoons until the timing was right for the farming. With Kayla just back in town and so many kids, they were prioritizing family time.

They entered the little porch room. "This is charming." A

white wicker loveseat and two oversized chairs sported matching cushions in white with blueberry plants laden with fruit. The combination of blues and greens was especially appealing. Leo set the tray on the wicker coffee table. Kristin noticed Mason jars full of iced water were already there, decorated with twine around them from the wedding.

Warmth filled her. That one piece of furniture reminded her of their first kiss at Miracle Mommies. Memories of last night's slow dancing made her toes curl. They'd had such a spectacular evening, and it made her want to spend as much time with the cowboy as possible.

He motioned where to sit on the loveseat and Kristin did. Then he cut off pieces of coffee cake and placed them onto plates with some fruit, one for each of them.

When he took the seat beside her, they were cozy their shoulders touched. Leo offered grace in just a few words, about the gift of Jesus on this day and asking for the strength to trust His hand to guide their lives. It was a bit unusual from other Christmas prayers she'd heard. She chimed in with "amen," and they dug in.

It still wasn't bright outside, and the windows looked out over the fields on the beauty of ice clinging to tree branches. "Sitting here with you is the best Christmas gift ever."

"We must be kindred spirits. We appreciate joining in with groups of people, yet need time with just the two of us. I wanted a little quiet time and hope you like it back here."

*I like you.*

She leaned in, appreciating the closeness, the safety of Leo's solidness. "I so enjoyed last night, spending the time with you and your family. They're great people. The kids are adorable, but it's the adults that are holding everything together. I admire you all so much."

He took a bite of coffee cake. "I had a good time, too, better than I expected, honestly. Your being there has everything to do with that. My family's something else, aren't they? Everything that happened got me thinking…"

"I know. During the vows, I wondered what it would be like to make that kind of commitment, to someone who is a soul mate. I've never experienced that." Since meeting Leo, she knew something had been missing with Craig, her ex husband.

When Leo leaned forward, she could see the gold flecks in his deep brown eyes and her heart rate kicked up. He said, "I thought about how much I adore you and want to be with you. I'm sorry I was hesitant at first."

She let that sink in as Leo finished the last bite, scooped up the remaining raspberries and ate them before setting his plate on the coffee table.

Kristin. had always considered him more than a brother but hadn't told him because she valued his friendship. She'd dreamed of this moment. "I know you've been concerned about me and uh, my situation, but a person can't change themselves for somebody else. I don't want you to feel I need rescued or something. I know what it's like when one person isn't on the same page."

"You don't understand. You're what I want. I've been called

a fixer. Well, your marriage didn't work out, but it wasn't your fault. You're perfect just the way you are."

She rested her hand over her heart and lay her head on his shoulder. "You have no idea how much I needed to hear that."

He took both of her hands in his. "God brought us to this place. You didn't want to be a single mom, and I didn't want to be a dad. But everything was meant for our good. You've made me see I don't want to be alone anymore."

Kristin had been listening so intently to Leo she hadn't seen two little ones come into the room in matching footed pajamas, one wearing green and one red. Ella climbed into her lap and Drew climbed into Leo's. Each snuggled in and dozed right off.

Leo patted Drew's back and Kristin's heart nearly melted when he said, "I'll love and cherish you, and your babies, too. I can see how my heart has wrapped around these two." He looked at his sleeping niece and nephew.

Without disturbing Drew, Leo reached under a cloth she hadn't noticed on the coffee table, and whipped out a small box. He lifted the lid, and the ring inside with a small diamond surrounded by tiny red stones looked like an antique.

"This was my grandmother's, and as the eldest, it was given to me. Kristin, will you marry me? These weeks we've been together have been the best of my life. With your pregnancy and getting over your past, we can have a long engagement. I'd just like to be married before the triplets are born. I promise to stay with you here in Fair Creek."

"I love you with all my heart, more than I've ever loved

anyone. Whatever happens, we'll face together, with God's help. But am I asking too much, because these babies won't be your biological children, Leo? Will you be able to love them and be their dad, even though you don't share the same DNA?"

"Seeing their mother reflected in them will be more than enough for me. Looks like I'll be doing Indiana farm scenes as the next phase of my career and that suits me fine. I'll love your children—our children—as my own. I already do."

He kissed her more tenderly than he ever had. The kiss was full of enough promise and hope to see them through the rest of their lives.

Continue to enjoy the town of Fair Creek and meet Gage Galloway and Bree Mason. Their story appears in:
*Her Billionaire Cowboy's Best Friend*
*Galloway Sons Farm*
*A Fair Creek Romance, Book 3*

# About the Author

Cathy Shouse writes inspirational cowboy romance. Her Fair Creek series, set in Indiana, features the Galloway brothers of Galloway Sons Farm. Much like the characters in her stories, Cathy once lived on a farm in "small town" Indiana where she first fell in love with cowboys while visiting the rodeo every summer.

Sign up to receive her newsletter at: www.cathyshouse.com where you'll get free books, exclusive bonus content, and news of her releases and sales.

If you liked this book, please take a moment to review it! Authors (including Cathy) really appreciate this, and it helps draw more readers to books they might like. Thanks!